The Legends of Leeper Holler Collection

AUTHOR OF URBAN LEGENDS OF LINCOLN COUNTY MISSOURI

THE LEGENDS OF LEEPER HOLLER COLLECTION

NORMAN MCFADDEN

THE LEGENDS OF LEEPER HOLLER COLLECTION

Norman McFadden

THE LEGENDS OF LEEPER HOLLER COLLECTION

This book is designed to provide accurate and authoritative information with regard to the subject matter covered. Certain stories contained within this work include fictitious characters.

Any similarity to real individuals is coincidental.

The opinions expressed by the author are not necessarily those of Polston House Publishing, LLC.

Published by Polston House Publishing LLC
www.PolstonHouse.com

Artwork used from public domain.

Published in the United States of America

CONTENTS

We hope that you enjoy the stories in this collection, from the books Legends of Leeper Holler 1 and 2. At the Author's request, we have made available this compilation for a special Halloween release. A hardback version will be available soon!

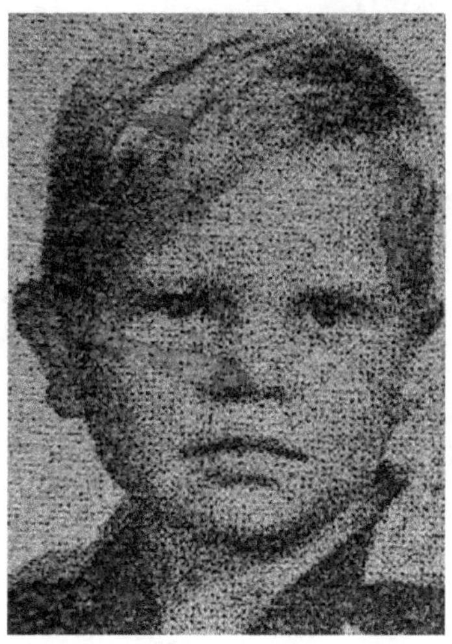

"Little Mac"Author Norman McFadden.

The Legends of Leeper Holler Collection

The Adventures of Little Mac

1

Grandpa The Moonshiner

It is 1964, and I'm a ten year old boy. My name is Little Mac and I live in the backwoods of Southeast Missouri. In a sleepy little town that lay along the mighty Black River, called Leeper. I actually live in Leeper Holler. I have adventures every day, since my mom always said, "Life is an adventure, so get out there and find it". I took her words to heart, and I get out there and live my life to its fullest every day.

Tomorrow is Saturday and my cousin Junior is spending the night with me. It's always a lot of fun running around with him. Because he is more than a cousin to me, he is my friend too. It was time to wake him up, so I gave him a great big kick, and out of the bed he flew! B-O-O-M!!, he hit the floor. He woke up quick when he hit the floor, and he looked up at me from where he landed.

"What in the sam hill did you do that for?" He asked.

I just started laughing.

"Okay, it is a little funny." He said as a big smile came across his face.

"So I'm up now and what have you got planned for us to do today?" He asked.

"Well the first thing we need to do is to get some food, but not waking up the whole house." I said. So we tiptoed into the kitchen and got some food out of the icebox. Then we wrote mom a note telling her that we were going down to see grandpa.

All the folk in Leeper Holler know my grandpa. And not just in Leeper, but in the whole county. They all know that old Charles Waist Laxton. He is the only moonshiner for 50 miles in any direction. And he has to work hard to stay up with the demand for it.

We decided to watch and follow grandpa back to his moonshine shed. We hid in the brush outside his house and watched for him to come out and head back into the woods. It was 7 a.m. and we sat there for 30 minutes watching his back door and eating our food. Finally we see the back door to his house open up, but we could not see who it was. A few seconds later we see my grandma come out and go to the chicken pen to get some eggs. And back into the house she went.

We knew the eggs were for grandpa to eat because he wouldn't eat anything that was not fresh. If it had been sitting on a store shelf, he didn't want it, he wouldn't even eat leftovers. We sat in the brush waiting about another 30 minutes. We were about to go out of our minds! Two young boys hiding, waiting, doing absolutely nothing but sitting quietly.

We were about ready to give up when the door finally opened and grandpa walked out. He had a big brown bag thrown up over one shoulder and a 12 gauge shotgun in the other hand. We knew he had used that shotgun before and even put people six foot under the ground, up beside the water tower. Much of the time, if he felt like someone was following him, he would just shoot over their head to scare them a little. Just to make them run away. The one he killed had found his moonshine still, and that was his livelihood! That was how he put food into his house, and no one messed with my grandpa's livelihood.

We followed from a good ways behind him so he could not see us. We went up and over one hill, two hills and three hills. We dropped off into the third big valley when grandpa began following a little creek up the valley.

We followed that little creek right to its end where it seemed to be running right under the side of the hill.

There was grandpa's still right next to the spring. We stayed back in the woods hiding behind two trees and just watched him working around the still. I had heard a lot about this spring; it is supposed to have healing power, the one and only healing spring. Grandpa was working with his still, carrying water from the spring and putting it into the top of the still. Then he opened a little tap on the bottom of the still and some kind of liquid come from the tap.

I knew, even at age 10, that was moonshine in the jugs. He put four or five jugs into the big bag he had brought with him. Then he sat three beside the still and picked up his shotgun in one hand and the big bag in the other hand. As soon as he got them in his hands, down the valley he headed. We watched until he went out of our sight.

As soon as we were sure that grandpa was gone, we both came from behind the trees and headed to the still.

The second Junior got there he picked up a jug of shine and said, “Hey Mac. are we going to drink some?”

I looked at him and said “Does a bear poop in the woods?”

He looked at me with a crazy look on his face as if to say, “What!”

I said “Yes Junior, why would we follow grandpa here just to look at the still.”

“Who is going first, you or me?” he asked.

I asked him if he had a penny so we could flip it and call heads or tails. Junior dug into his pockets and pulled out two pennies.

“We only need but one.” I replied.

He gave me one of the pennies and I said, “Call it.” as I threw it into the air. He called heads. I caught it in one hand placed it over the other hand, and then took my hand off and called out, “You got it, it’s heads.”

“I’m first.” Junior said looking a little bit nervous. “But it doesn't matter what happens to me because after I drink it you still have to drink some, too.”

I replied, “I will. Don’t you worry 'bout it!”

“You're not going to do it, are you?” Junior asked me.

Junior was so nervous that I wasn’t going to drink too that we decided to go together on the count of three. We opened two of the jugs that grandpa had set on the ground and counted slowly to three.. “Now here we go; one, two, three!” And up the jugs went to our lips. The moonshine poured into our mouths at right exactly the same time.

Oh God, it burned my mouth so much I wanted to scream and shout! When it made it’s way to our throats it felt like we had swallowed a ball of fire! I didn't think it would feel as bad when it hit my belly. Boy was I wrong! the worst feeling was as it settled down to our bellies. I looked at Junior and his face was as red as a poker just out of a blazing fire. He had tears in his eyes, and I had never seen Junior cry anytime that I had been with him before. The second it hit my belly, I started to cough and gag.

"Junior, I think I'm dying." I managed to sputter.

"Me too." He said between his coughing and gagging.

We both got the idea at the same time, we ran and jumped into the cold water of the spring and started drinking the water as fast as we could. We found out real fast that this just made it worse. I heard someone laughing at us, so we turned and looked around, and we could see that it was grandpa!

He stopped laughing just long enough to say, "Now I'm going to have to kill you both." To my surprise, he pointed his shotgun right at me and said, "If I'm lucky maybe I can kill both of you with one shot."

I thought I was going crazy! My own grandpa was saying that he was going to shoot me, and hide my body somewhere it will never be found!

To my total surprise, Junior said, "Go head shoot me, put me out of my misery! If you don't kill me your moonshine will! But it will kill me slowly."

Grandpa turned the shotgun away from me and pointed it at Junior, and to my surprise, he pulled the trigger! I thought my heart had stopped for a second as

Junior stumbled and fell back into the cold water of the spring. Grandpa started laughing again and said, “I'm not going to kill you, but you both got to promise not tell anyone where my still is. And no Christmas or birthday presents for you this year.”

Junior looked a little funny and said, “But you don’t get me any Christmas or birthday presents.”

Grandpa replied, “I do now and here is $5 for each of you and I’ll walk you boys back to town.”

So he walked us to town and we bought so much candy we got sick and decided maybe moonshine and candy don't mix. Three days later we walked back to grandpa's still, but it was completely gone. I guess you never know someone as well as you think you do!

2

Elbow Room

It was a cold October 29th, in 1961. Little Mac was waking up as he rolled out of bed and hit the floor with a thump. He was 8 years old and shared a bed with his sister Kathy, who could kick like a donkey in her sleep. It was about 6:00am. and he could hear his mother in the other room cooking some breakfast. So he got up off the floor and walked into the other room and sat down at the table. Little Mac had decided that it was time for him and Mom to have a talk about the sleeping arrangements.

He started by saying, "Mom I'm getting too big to be sleeping with my sister". His mom stopped cooking and looked at him, she realized that he was getting pretty big. "Ok," she said, "Tonight you will start sleeping with your brother Dave."

My first thought was, 'Oh no, not Dave!' You have to understand that Dave is like the devil, and he has a way of making my life a living hell. He was the meanest kid in the whole world, no joke at all.

I cried, "Oh no Mom, not Dave. Kenny or Charles, but please not Dave."

She walked over to me bent down and kissed my forehead. With a smile she said, "You will be alright." But I had my doubts about that.

We all used to sleep in the same room, the whole family. Mom, dad, my sister, my three brothers and me in one little room. My mom thought about our conversation that morning and went to my dad. She told dad that she needed some elbow room, that it was just too many people in one room. So my dad had the bright idea that since he worked at the local sawmill he would bring home some of the scrap slabs and build us boys our own room.

Now let me tell you about that room that my dad built for us boys. It seemed like a great idea at the moment, but it turned out to be a real bad idea. Oh it was great until the bark fell off the slabs, and then the rain, snow, and wind would come right though the holes in the walls.

So dad got another clever idea, "I'll just get some cardboard boxes, flatten them out and put them over the holes in the wall."

Well that worked until the cardboard got wet, then it fell apart too. Dad had no more ideas on the matter, and the snow, rain and wind continued to blow through our bedroom. I only have three words to describe it. “IT WAS HELL”. Only unlike hell, it was cold. We could not even leave a glass of water sitting out in our room, or else it would freeze solid.

It was hard but we grew up with a sincere respect for what we have now. And we learned not to look down on people who have nothing.

3

Doc Hurley and The James Gang

It was half past five on Saturday morning. All the world was bright and brimming with life. Everyone was still asleep but me, little Mac. I'm heading out to go next door to see my old buddy, Doc Hurley. Doc Rode with the Jesse James Gang, or so he said. Old Doc was about ninety or so and no one knew for sure, but I loved that old man.

I got to Doc's door at the same time every Saturday. I knocked on the door and he said, "Come on in Mac. Pull up a seat and park your butt." So I came on in and sat down and old Doc began asking me things like, "Hey, little Mac, would you like a cup of good old moonshine?"

"Oh no Doc, just a cup of milk would do me fine." I would say. "How about some buttermilk biscuits with your milk?" He would holler with the door to his icebox open. Doc's biscuits were so hard that you could throw them at a rabbit and kill it!

But I always went home from Doc's with both of my pockets full of his homemade biscuits. So you know I said "Yes-sir-ee-bob!" to the biscuits. Old Doc got the milk and the biscuits and set them on the table beside me. Then he walked back to the old wood burning stove to get his. Now old Doc didn't like milk, and he kept it around just for me. He came back to the table with his biscuit and a cup of my grandpa's homemade moonshine. We would just sit and talk and sometimes he would tell me a story about when he rode with Jesse James. On this day, he told me how it came to be that he was called by the name of Doc. This is his story.

"It was September of 1872 and I was at the Kansas City Fair. There were a lot of people there and I was just another face in the crowd. I was about 13 year old, well I would be come December. It was later that afternoon when three men approached the ticket taker. I could see their guns were out so I walked a little closer to see what was going on. One of the men fired his gun at the ticket taker. The shot missed him, and hit a young girl in the leg.

They took the money from the ticket man and rode off. I found my horse and followed them but stayed a ways back so not to be seen. I followed them for about a day and then we entered Clay County. They headed up into a big holler. I knowed that I shouldn't have followed them into that holler but I did. Steep hills on both sides made it near impossible to go up with a horse. Only two ways to go, the way I was going, or to turn around and go back. So I just keep on going the way I was going up the holler. I rode right into a dead end, so now I could only turn and go back. I turned and headed back the way I came and thought I lost them.

I had just gone a little way further when I saw them, but they saw me too. I had no place to run, one of the men rode right up beside me with his gun pointing at me. He turned around and looked at the two men and shouted, "Hey, it's just a kid." Then he looked back at me and said, "I'm Jesse James, so who the sam hill are you, and why are you following us? Are you trying to get yourself killed?" I just looked at him at a total loss for words.

He said "Cat got your tongue, boy?"

I looked down at the ground and said, "I'd like to ride with you, I've got no home to go back to Mr. James."

" 'Mr', He said, "I like the sound of that!" Then he turned to the two men who were with him and said, "Hey, we could use a house boy to cook and clean couldn't we?" Jesse looked back at me and said, "Come on, but we all gonna be keeping an eye on you."

We rode about ten miles from the holler to a big cave, and we rode right up into it on the horses. About a half a mile back in the cave it seemed to really open up. A little house was sitting beside one wall of the cave. The man that didn't speak took our horses and we went inside the house.

Jesse said with a smile on his face "Here it is, home sweet home. Now get to work, I'm hungry!"

So I did just what he said, and cooked them a good meal. "Oh! I didn't tell you how I got the name Doc did I? See I used to help my dad on the farm to doctor up cows when they got hurt. One time a cow got shot and I had to help dad dig out the bullet. Well the boys would come in from a job all shot up sometimes and I got to doctoring Jesse's gang up. They begun calling me Doc and I liked the sound of it, so I just told everyone I met to call me Doc."

"Well, That's all of this story, but next Saturday I'll tell you how I ended up in Leeper Holler." So I said my goodbye. But I'll see him next week, if God is willing, for another Jesse James adventure.

Well my five days at school just seemed to fly by and I was in school just keep thinking about riding with the James gang. What fun it had to be for a kid, I bet it was so cool being there, Doc was so lucky. I went to sleep Friday night thinking and dreaming all about Jesse James, and the adventures they had. I woke up Saturday and couldn't wait to get to Doc's house.

I got to the door and knocked, and I could hear Doc on the inside cooking and singing some old song I never heard before. It was something about Jim Danny it sound like it come from the 1800's or something.

“Come on in Mac, sit down and take the weight off your feet.” So I came on in and pushed up a bucket and sat down at the table. “Hey Mac would you like some milk and some biscuits? They’re buttermilk biscuits!” Doc said with a big smile, like to say thanks for coming over and keeping a lonely old man company. He was standing at his old wood burning cooking stove with a cup of milk in one hand and in the other a plate of homemade biscuits. He sat them on the table in front of me and said, “Help yourself.”

He turned back to the icebox to get a jug of moonshine out of it. He came back to the table with a jug of moonshine in one hand and a tin cup in the other hand. As he sat down he said, “Back to the story of how I ended up here in Leeper, Missouri. Well I’d been with the James gang about a year or maybe more, I was turning 14 years old.

Jesse came in and looked at me and said, “Doc, your almost a man now. How would like to go on a job with us?”

I replied, “I would love it, but I don’t have a gun.”

Jesse smile and said, “And you don’t need one, you just a cook for us. It’s goin’ to be a three day trip. We all goin’ to go down south to a little town called Gasp Hills and goin’ to camp out at the Black River. That camp is about 15 mile from the job and that’s the closest you are goin’ to get to the job.”

“Come on Jesse give me a break I’m almost a man, you just said it yourself.” I explained. All the men were sittin’ around the table just to watch us argue.

Cole Younger said “He got you there Jesse.” And all the men began to laugh. Jesse said “Alright kid you asked for it. We will all go to the Black River to make camp. Doc you’re not wanted anywhere so as we are making camp you can go to a little town called Leeper and get food for four days.”

So we packed everything we could carry on our horses, and rode out going south. It took three days of hard riding to get to our campsite on the great Black River.

When we got to the campsite Jesse said to me, "Ride back to the train tracks we passed a little bit ago, and go south along them for a mile 'til you come to Leeper."

So I just got on my horse a headed on over to town to get food for us. It took me about one hour, and by the time I got back, they had already made camp. As I rode up Jesse took a 30 minute break and then got our horses unloaded and I started cooking. We all ate and got ourselves to bed. Tomorrow was going to be a big day, it was Doc’s first job. Everyone was asleep quick except for the lookout.

The next day we were up before the sun. Jesse told Cole Younger “We need someone to watch the camp. And shut your mouth about Doc going with us. It’s going to be your job to watch the camp, maybe you will keep you mouth closed next time.” Cole didn’t say anything, he just threw a piece of wood at the ground a walked away. The rest of us got our horses ready to go.

Jesse told Cole that we should be back five or six hours. If not, then close up camp and head back home.

Cole simply replied, “Ok.”

With that we rode off. In two hours we got to Gasp Hills, then we rode about five minutes south on the railroad tracks. Where we stopped, there was a big hill each side of the track. Jesse told everyone what to do.

My job was to get on one side of the track and roll some big rocks down onto the tracks. And then wait there as they got on the train then they would wave at me when they came back out of the train. Everything had to be perfect, the train had shipment of gold on it.

Soon after we got ready I heard the train whistle blowing. I rolled the big rocks on to the track as Jesse had told me to. The train was coming up the track fast! The man who was driving saw the rocks on the track, so he put the brake on. The train stopped about a foot from the rocks, some workers jumped out of the front of the train and as they jumped out, Jesse and the boys jumped on to the back of the train.

I could see it all clear from where I was sitting. The men from the train started moving the rocks from the train track. It took ten minutes to get the track cleared and the men headed back to the train. I keep looking for Jesse and the boys to get off the train but they hadn’t. I thought to myself hurry up Jesse. The train was starting to move again. About that time, jumping off the train with bags in his hands was Jesse and the boys with four more brown bags.

Jesse waved at me to get on my horse and ride down the back side of the hill and meet them at the bottom of it. By the time I got down the hill, I saw Jesse and the boys waiting for me already on the horses. We rode off as Jesse said, "Good job! When a shots not fired at all, it's a great job!" We rode back to our camp on Black River. When we rode up, Cole said, "You all are back in four hours, good job."

I got off my horse and started cooking. It had been a long day and we were all hungry. After we ate, Jesse again told all of us, "Good job men, but we got a long way to go to get back home." I was thinking that we need to hide the gold somewhere before we ride on home. So I told the guys what was on my mind. "There is going to be a lot of lawmen looking for this gold. I was thinking that we were better off without it. Especially if we got stopped along the way home." "Maybe we should hide it." Jesse suggested. We all said okay, but that Jesse should be the one to hide it. So Jesse took one load and headed into the woods, that was the first of four trips. It took about ten minutes every time, so it had to be pretty close to our camp. After that we all just sat around and took it easy.

A little later Cole was cleaning his gun, and it went off hitting me right in the shoulder. The bullet went in the front and out the back of my shoulder.

Jesse cried out, "Oh God Cole, you are such a dummy."

I was bleeding bad. Frank got a clean rag and wrap my shoulder up. "Jesse," Frank said, "What are we going to do?"

Jesse said "Let me think….I got it. Doc, you know the little place where you got the food from?" I replied "Yes!"

"Cole will ride with you to that town because he is the dummy that got you hurt. You can just stay in Leeper and when we come back to get the gold we will get you."

So we said goodbye, then me and Cole took off. The pain was the worst I had ever had in my life. The 15 minute ride seemed like a lifetime.

When we got to the doctor's house and Cole said, "I can't go in with you because I'm wanted by the law, I've got a poster on me."

I said, "Okay". He told me how sorry he was and he hoped things would go well for me. With that he rode off. I told the doctor I had a hunting accident. He took it at that and took me in, and cared for me like his own son for three years. I worked hard, and when I was 18 I got this house, but I never saw Jesse again. I heard that he went to his house, to his wife and kids, and got shot and killed by one of his own men.

I looked for that gold all my life. I dug over 10,000 holes in the woods near the campsite we had so many years ago. I never to this day found that gold. It's still up there waiting for someone to find it. Now you know how I got to this town of Leeper, Missouri.

I do not know how many you had hurt: I do know how happy you made a lonely boy. How you charged his life with your stories, how you made him love you with his whole heart! Rest easy and may God open His doors for this old man that helped a boy to grow into a good man.

-Love you Doc!

4

The Joke that Killed

It is 1963, I'm 10 years old. It's a cold and snowy afternoon in a southern town in the backwoods of Missouri. A little boy is out playing with friends on the snowy hillside. I'm the boy that they call Little Mac. The other boys I'm playing with are my cousin Junior who had spent the night with me, and two other boys are named Ricky and Cecil. Ricky and Cecil are both a big bully and a joker.

We were sledding on the biggest hill in Leeper Holler. Every time we would slide down the hill we would end up right in blind John's front yard. John is an old blind man who lives by himself, he would often ask the kids of Leeper Holler to run to town for him. John had heard us playing outside and was waiting for the next boy to come down the hill.

So as Ricky slid down the hill and into John's front yard, John called out to Ricky, "Hey would you go to town for me? I'll pay you."

Ricky ran over to talk to John, now we could not hear what they were saying, but we saw Ricky go to the side of the house and pick up a five gallon can. A minute or two later Ricky came walking up the hill to where we were all standing at the top.

He said to us, "John asked me to run to town for him and get him some kerosene so that he can get his fire started tonight. And he gave me a whole dollar to do it."

Cecil said, "I got a great joke we can play on old John."

"What?" Said Ricky. Junior and I just stood there listening as Cecil was explaining the joke to us. "We go to town and fill his kerosene can full of gasoline and when he tries to start his fire tonight the gas will explode at him."

"That will scare the old mad to death. Is that going to be funny?" I asked.

Ricky said, "That will be funny!"

I said, "I don't think it's a good idea, he could get hurt or something."

As I was objecting, Ricky walked up behind me and grabbed both of my arms and pulled them behind my back. Cecil walked over to me and hit me right in the nose and said, "If you babies tell anyone about our plan we will give you both some more of this." My nose was bleeding pretty bad, so I got handful of snow and put it on my nose in hopes of stopping the bleeding. Junior asked me if I was alright? I told him that I would be fine.

Junior and I got our sleds and left because we didn't want any part of those plans. On the way home we were talking about how many ways their plan could go wrong and someone could get hurt.

I asked Junior, "Do you think we should tell someone?"

Junior replied about as fast as I said it, "No way! They can and will hurt us bad. They were not playing about beating us up. No way, no, I am not telling anyone."

I was so angry by his answer. By the time we got to my house it was time to eat, and after we ate it was too late to go back out and play. So we sat around playing games until it was time to go to bed at 9:00 pm. My three brothers had the bed taken up that night, so Junior and I decided to make a bed in the living room. But that was cool with us because Dave had his friend staying the night. Dave and his friend were two of the meanest boys you have ever seen. So we needed to stay as far away from them as we could.

We didn't go right to bed. We fixed up a cot on the floor and then told some jokes. We were laughing so loud that mom and dad had to tell us to be quiet around ten. After that we decided that maybe it was time to get some sleep.

Around midnight, Junior and I woke up to someone hammering loud on the front door. We were the first ones awake because we were on the floor in the front room. I got up quick to see who it was and was surprised to find Ricky's dad there.

He asked me to go get my dad up as fast as I could. So I ran into the other room to get mom and dad. I told them that he was at the door wanting them to come right away. I followed my dad to the door so that I could listen to them talk.

He told my dad, "Blind John's house is on fire and he is still in it. We could hear him calling out for help."

Dad ran into his bedroom to get some clothes on quick. So I told Junior that we ought to get dressed and go check it out. We got going as fast as we could and followed dad up the road to John's house.

By the time we got there the house was totally engulfed by the fire. Junior hit me on the shoulder as he saw Ricky and Cecil coming our way.

"Oh no. It's time for us to go back home now." But it was too late, they were already following us. I slowed down and let them catch up with us because I had something I had to say to those two jokers.

Before they could say a word I got in Ricky's face and told him, "You know that if John got burned up in that fire it is your fault. You two are the reason this happened."

Cecil said "The old man did burn up, and me and Ricky don't care, not even a little bit. We killed John and if you boys tell even one person, just one, we will get you and douse you in gas and burn you up just like we did him!"

Junior and I knew that they would, because they were both was as crazy as bed bug. So blind John died that night and nobody knew the truth until now. It's too late to get justice for John but it not too late to get it out of my head.

When a joke hurts someone, that is when the joke stops being funny!

-John this is for you!

5

The

Nipper Woods

Bigfoot

I got up before any of my family was awake and I tip-e-toed through the house. I looked at my three brothers sleeping and was thinking to myself what I could do to get back at Dave. Dave was one of my older brothers who had made it his life's mission to make me miserable.

There's a nasty mud hole out back in the pig pen. So I walked out back and got a handful of mud and tip-e-toed back into the house. I walked past my mom and dad sleeping, and my sister Kathy. I walked back into my brother's room with some stinky mud in one hand and holding my nose with the other. Dave always slept in his under pants so his pants were lying by his bed. I picked up the pants as quiet as I could and filled one leg full of the mud and sneaked back out of the house. I was headed next door to my good friend Doc Hurley's house.

Old Doc was about 90, and was the town drunk. But I loved the old man, he was a good friend to a lonely 10 year boy. As I walked into his house he was cooking on an old wood stove. He said, "Hey little Mac, would you like something to eat? Pull up a bucket and sit down." Doc didn't have any chairs just some old buckets to sit on.

So I pulled up a bucket and sat down. Doc asked what was going on so I told him about what I had done to Dave and we both had a good laugh about it. He sat down a plate of bacon and eggs, with a biscuit on the side. His biscuits were so hard you could kill a rabbit with them, so I stuck the biscuit in my pocket rather than eating it.

As we started eating, someone knocked at the front door. His house was a shotgun home, which means you walk in the front door and arrive at the back door in just a few steps. So Doc got up and headed for the front door. I could hear him call out to ask who was there, then he said, "It's not locked, come on in and stop the darn knocking before you wake the whole town up!" He got to the front door at the same time it flew open and hit him right in the head. As he shook his head and let out some bad words, I tried to stifle my laughter and heard him say, "Oh it's you!" It was Tuffy.

Tuffy was an old one-armed man that lived up at the edge of Leeper. He was a wino and the people didn't like him much.

They would go the other way so they wouldn't have to see or talk to him. But he was my friend and I loved to hear him tell his stories. He was a great storyteller, especially about ghosts and other unearthly terrors in the dark.

One thing about Tuffy, he was always in a hurry. He came running into Doc's house talking fast like he always did. Asking if me and Doc would go pick some blackberries with him. See Tuffy was wanting to make a blackberry cobbler and that sounded just fine to Doc, so he said that was a good idea. Then he said, "Little Mac would like to go along with us?" I told him that I would have to go and ask my mom. Tuffy told me I had better make it fast because he was wantin' to get going.

I started out the door then turned back and asked where we were going to pick blackberries at. Tuffy said we were going to the nipper woods. As I got to the back door of my house I could hear mom cooking inside. I was trying to think of how I could word my question so she would let me go with them.

I thought I had it, so in I went. After I gave my mom a kiss and said good morning I jumped right in… "Mom, them crazy old men are going into the nipper woods to look for blackberries, and I know if them two men go by themselves they could get hurt bad. They need me to go just to keep an eye on them!" The moment I looked into her eyes I knew she wasn't buying my story.

She said, "Little Mac go tell Tuffy and Doc it would be a cold day in hell before I let my 10 year old boy go with them across the street much less five miles to the nipper woods to spend the day alone with them. Have I got stupid written across my forehead?!?!"

So with my head hanging down, I went next door to Doc's house and with a sad tone in my voice said "Sorry guys I can't go, Mom's got work for me to do today." Tuffy and Doc were sorry that I couldn't go, since they could have used the extra hands. They were really anxious to get started so they would be able to make it back before dark. They grabbed a couple of buckets and were on their way, without me. And I headed home.

All day long I kept on thinking about how much fun Doc and Tuffy must be having without me. The day drug on and I could hardly wait to talk to Tuffy and Doc to see how their day was. It was getting dark and still no word from them. I was getting worried. I walked around and sat on the front porch. I stared down the road and tried to see through the darkness. The road was as silent as a graveyard.

Then I heard someone talking and I could tell by the voice that it was Tuffy! I could see Tuffy in front and Doc was lagging behind. Tuffy's shirt was torn and hanging off of him in shreds. Doc was as white as a ghost. Tuffy was talking a lot but Doc was not saying a word. As they got closer to me I asked what had happened? Tuffy murmured, “It was not a ghost, it was something else.”

He told me to walk over to Doc’s and have a seat on the porch so he could tell me all about it. As we sat down he began talking about the strange happenings of the day. When they arrived at the nipper woods they found a big old blackberry path and begun picking blackberries as fast as their hands could go.

They didn’t even stop to take a drink of wine. Right about the time they had the bucket almost full of berries they heard something heading down the hill! Each step made the ground shake, so they sat down to take a better look around. Berries were toppling from the bucket as the ground shook. Doc said “Tuffy! Let’s get behind that big tree there!”

So they hid behind the tree and when they sneaked a peek out from behind the tree, they saw it.

“What did you see, what was it?” I asked.

“It was as big as a mountain, and it had more hair on it’s body than my ex-girlfriend had on her, and she had hair everywhere. She could even grow a better beard than I could.” Tuffy said.

Still Doc hadn’t said a word, not one word! Tuffy just kept talking. He said as it got closer, we could see it was a Bigfoot! It got to the blackberry path and saw there was no blackberries left on the bush. It walk over where the berries had fell from our bucket and picked them up off the ground and ate them right down. It looked right at us like the tree was not there at all.

It let out a growl that shook the hat right off of my head. Doc got real scared, and threw his whole bucket of berries down at the Bigfoot's feet. The Bigfoot was not happy just having Doc's berries, he came right up to me and growled in my face so hard my fake teeth fell out of my mouth on to the ground!

As I stood there toothless I thought to myself, if I don't give him my berries he is going to get me. So I threw my berries at his feet and he sat down on the ground to eat my berries I had worked so hard for. I took off as fast as I could only looking for a second to see what Doc was doing.

He was standing there like a frozen man, and as white as one too. But I kept running as fast as I could through the berry path. The thorns were pulling at my shirt and tearing it to threads! As I got on the other side of the berry path, I was running so fast I couldn't slow down for the big hill and I fell head over heels as I got the bottom of the hill.

I came to rest as my head hit a big rock knocking me out. A little later I woke up thinking, where my buddy Doc was at. The last time I saw him he was at the tree face to face with Bigfoot. So I got up and ran back to the top of the hill and headed in the berry path again. I got to the other side of the berry path. I could see Doc still standing in the same place with the same look on his face, and not moving at all.

I tried to talk to him, but he would not move at all. And he is still not talking. I looked at Doc and Tuffy and I said, "I've got it, just wait here I'll be right back."

I ran into Doc's house and got his moonshine out and poured a cup of it and headed back off to see Doc and Tuffy on the porch. I told Tuffy, "With your good arm hold his top lip up."

With one hand I held the cup of moonshine, with the other I pried his mouth open. As he opened up I poured his mouth full of the moonshine. As he swallowed the shine he began to wake up and get his color back. He said "Tuffy are we going to go and pick some blackberries or not?"

Tuffy said "We did go!"

Doc said "Have you gone crazy? We have not gone to get berries!"

We told him the whole story but he never remembered it.

Like it hadn't happened at all.

Norman Mcfadden

6

The First Day of School

It is 1959 and I am a 6-year-old boy. It's the first day of school and I'm so excited! I can't wait to make some new friends. Leeper Holler is so small...like 10 kids in the whole holler, and half of them are family. We have to be at school by 7 a.m so we have to get up at 4:30 a.m. We have to do our chores before we can get dressed in our school clothes.

Today is my brother Dave's turn to feed the pigs but he said it's not his turn. My big brother Charles could do it, but he works. Mom and Dad said he has a car and a girlfriend, he has to work for the money for them. Oh..I almost forgot to tell you my job. I had to feed and water the rabbits, a great job today.

By the time we all get done with our work – the pigs and the chickens and rabbits and fetching the water, Mom would have breakfast on the table, so we could all eat together. As soon as we finish eating, it is time to get dressed for school. I just could not wait to get to school and make new friends!

By this time it was getting close to 6 a.m. To get to school it took about 45 minutes to walk there. Mom would have our bag lunches sitting on the table waiting for us. It didn't matter which one you took because they all were the same - we all had a peanut butter sandwich and a jug of water.

We all grabbed our lunches and headed down the road for the long walk to school. Mom stopped me for just a minute and told me, "You have new clothes on, not hand-me-downs, so try not to get them in a mess."

"Okay." I said. And was thinking if I can stay away from my brother Dave I will be able to stay clean. I walked with my sister, Kathy, so I don't have to deal with him right now. Kathy and I were walking ahead because Dave had to go up the holler from our house to get his friend, little boy. That was the only name I knew him by. He was about as bad as Dave, but then no one could be THAT bad.

Suddenly, I feel a big hard hit to the back of my head. It had to be Dave and that little boy behind us. 'I'm going to get it now', I thought. Dave yelled at me because

I was with the girls, "I knew you were a girl. I bet you have sit to pee, don't you little girl." He hit me on the head again; I thought I saw stars this time. About that time, Tom ran by and I said to my sister, good! because I knew there was one person in town Dave and 'little boy' loved picking on more than me, and it was Tom.

They took off after him. "Thank God." I said to myself. Maybe I can get to school with out getting beaten-up. We walked about a half a mile farther and I saw Dave and little boy by a well and Tom was naked as a jaybird. Dave and little boy had taken Tom's clothes off and put them in the well. Tom was crying, holding his hands over his boy parts. I felt sorry for him but was not going to say anything about it, or my new clothes would be in the well too. I just walked on with Kathy and got myself to school. Glad that I was still wearing clean clothes for now.

I stayed in school and didn't go outside to play at recess time with all the other kids because I don't want to run into Dave outside. I could just think of all the things he could do to me out there, and thought, "No thanks. I'll just stay in here where it is safe."

It was lunch time and we all ate our lunches. Dave is as crazy as a bedbug, but not crazy enough to do something in the school. Right after lunch I needed to go to the outdoor bathroom. I was thinking to myself, maybe I can hold it because it's just three hours more. The first 10 minutes were not bad, but it was beginning to stink like a polecat had gotten into the schoolhouse. I lifted my hand and told Miss Read, our teacher, that I had to go. She was the teacher for all six grades so she had no time to go with me. She told my cousin, Junior, "Your cousin, Little Mac, needs to go the bathroom so please go with him." Junior asked, "Why?" with a funny look on his face. Miss Read said, "Because he is new here and I said TO!"

"Okay," Junior said. But you could tell by the look on his face he was not happy. We walked out of the classroom and entered a long hall way. As we walk down the hall Junior said, "Nothing against you, but your crazy brother Dave is at recess now. You know how he is!" I looked at him and said, "Yes, I'm sorry to say I do!"

We got to the doors of the school. We looked out the glass of the doors looking for Dave or 'little boy'. We couldn't see them anywhere, but we knew that they were around somewhere. So we headed outside, we walked slowly and looked around like we were looking out for a pack of wolves in the grass. We got to the bathroom alright but I told Junior, "Stand watch in case my brother shows up."

I went in to do my business, but after about a second or two Junior was knocking at the door and crying "Let me in. I'm not going stay out here and let Dave kill me." I opened the door and let him in, "Hurry up before he gets here!" he said with a sad look on his face. Just then we heard a noise outside the door. It was Dave and little boy, we were both so scared. We heard him locking the door from the outside. He said, "Hey little girls, we will see you after school and then we heard a laugh.

I got finished as quick as I could and tried running into the door to break the lock off but it didn't work.

Junior put his head in his hands and said, "I just knew something like this would happen."

I said, "Let me think a second, just a second. Okay, I've got it!" I said.

"What have you got, just what have you got?" Junior asked with a cry. I said, "We can crawl down though the toilet hole to the big hole in the back of the outhouse. But, we will have to take off our clothes because if I get my clothes dirty I'm dead."

He finally agreed, "Okay." We took off our clothes and began to slide down the dark hole looking for light in the back of the cistern.

Slow and easy, step-by-step we went down. One wrong step and we would be up to our knees in poo and would smell like polecats. Junior cried out, "There is a wasps nest in here." About that time, one got on him and he fell on me and I fell into the poo, with Junior right on top of me.

We crawled out of the back with poo on every inch of our naked bodies. We both ran around to the front to get our clothes but the door was open and our clothes were gone. We heard Dave laughing so we looked to where the laughter was coming from. We saw Dave and 'little boy' with our clothes in their hands.

"Hey look at this," Dave said, as they tossed our clothes on top the school roof as we both cried "NO." There we were, naked and covered with poo from our heads to our toes!

All I could think about was what Mom was going to do to me if my clothes got torn up, but right now I'm going have to think about walking by all the kids on the playground and then walking into the classroom with poo all over our naked... "Let's get this over with." I cried.

We began walking by the kids on the playground. Little Sue was the first one to see us. She cried out to all the other kids, "Look at Little Mac. And, Junior is naked, too."

They all looked around at us laughing and pointing. We walked as fast as we could to get into the school, as fast as possible! We made it to the long hallway, and it seemed like an hour to walk that hallway with the kids outside fighting to look into glass doors to see our nude butts. We finally got to the classroom, a trip that seemed like a lifetime. As we walked into the classroom, all the kids heads turned our way as they began laughing and pointing at us. We hung our heads and thought we were going to be dead. At that time, Miss Read turned around from the blackboard and I though her eyes were going to hit the floor.

She started crying, "No-no-no, in the hallway now!" We headed back to the hallway and all the kids were still looking through the glass in the doors. When Miss Read got to the hallway, she saw the kids looking though the windows and ran them off. "Now," she said, "What is going on?"

We both just said not a word! She said, "Okay Junior, you are the oldest so start talking now." He finally told her the story and I just nodded my head to say that was the way it happened. Miss Read said, “Okay, we got to get you boys cleaned up and your clothes off the roof.”

After we got all that done, she looked at us with a smile on her face. “Now it’s time for Dave and ‘little boy’ to get their just dues.”

I didn’t like sound of that because what ever is done to him, he was going to give it back to me three times over. When school was out I had not made any new friends, but I did get a song made up about me and I didn’t like it at all.

On the good side of it, my new clothes didn’t get dirty.

That was Little Mac's first day of school. How was yours?

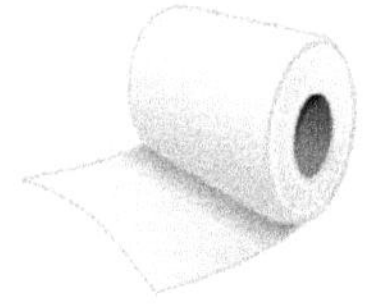

7

The Boy on All Fours

My great uncle Ben owned a bar that sat on the biggest hill in Leeper, overlooking the whole town. Ben use to say, "This bar is my throne, and the whole town around it is my foot stool." He was a good man, but just a little bit crazy. All the people of Leeper loved him and would have trusted him with their life. Until it happened and it drove him mad, and he had to be put away in the crazy house.

Well let me tell you the story. It was a cold December evening, two days before Christmas. As snow was falling on the sleepy little town, Ben was getting ready to close the bar for the night. He got all the money he made that day, and he put it in a brown bag and locked up the bar. Walking to his old car he was nearly shivering in the wind. Only three people in Leeper owned a car, and he was one of them.. As he got to the car he looked at the road and was thinking it's a lot of snow to try to drive down that big hill.

He got in anyway because it was too cold to walk home. He started up the car, and hadn't hardly gone anywhere when the car slid off into the ditch. It plowed right into a tree, and he hit his head hard on the windshield.

A big ole knot was already coming up on his head. Ben got out of the car and looked at it for a minute shaking his head. "I guess I'm going to have to walk home." Ben told himself. It was only about a mile if he take the short cut though the flat woods. So he got his money and a flashlight, and headed off to his house. About the middle of the big hill, he shone his light into the woods looking for a tiny path that ran straight though the flat woods to Leeper holler.

A smile came across his face, thinking about the stories people told about the flat woods. But he knew people didn't walk in the flat woods at night, and it would save him a mile. So down the narrow, dark, spooky pathway he went. His flashlight in one hand and a bag of money in the other, Ben also had his .38 in the bag with the money.

After he got just a few minutes into the woods, he heard something behind him. Ben turned to get a looks at whatever was following him. He saw something, but he thought it was just the darkness playing tricks on him. So he turned around and started walking again with the noises still back behind him. He started walking faster and whatever that was behind him started waking faster too.

Ben took his .38 from the bag and turned around suddenly. There it was! It was a boy about 18 years old and he was on all fours, with only had a rag covering his private parts up. His hair was as black as the dark night. His eyes were shining in the dark as the flashlight hit them, they were wild looking, like wolf eyes!

Ben said with a puzzled look on his face, "I don't know what you think you going to get, but I know what I'm going to give you, if you don't turn around a go away RIGHT NOW!" The boy just looked at Ben and moved his head from side to side as if to say, "I don't understand what you are saying to me.'

Ben didn't care, he was cold and just needed to get home with his bag of money. So he turned around and started walkin' away from the boy, because he didn't want to have to shoot a kid. He began to run on the path to just get home. The boy began running too. Ben had finally had enough. He stopped and turned around, he shot him three times and the boy fell and rolled a little down the hill.

Ben said to his self "I got him; I'll come back and check up on him tomorrow." With that he turned and again started walking home. but in less than five minutes, he heard something let out a howl! Then there was more howling. There was three, four, or maybe five wolves! He turned around to see. It was the boy leading a pack of wolves and they looked vicious, growling and showing their teeth, and they were coming right after him. "Oh God what have I done?" He thought out loud.

So he turned and ran as fast as his legs would carry him. He knew they were getting closer to him, but he did not turn around again, he just kelp running. He came off the path into Leeper Holler, and the first place he saw was Doc's house. So he ran up and started hammering on the door. He could still hear the boy and the wolves coming through the woods.

He was thinking, 'If I don't get in that house they are going to kill me. If I just walk in, Doc could shoot me, he could shoot me but the boy and them wolves are going to kill me, I just know it.' So with that he opened the door, and ran into the house. He closed the door behind him, and locked it as fast as he could!

By this time old Doc had got up with his shotgun in his hands. "What the cotton pickins going on here?" Doc said, with a mad look across his face. By that time the boy and the wolves were at his house, and were biting and scratching at the door, trying to get in.

Old Doc smiled and said "Friends of yours Ben?"

Ben said "Not any friends of mine Doc!"

Ben told Doc the story about the boy on his all fours but Doc wasn't buying it. Until he looked out the window in the back room and saw the wolves at the back door. Doc said “Well Ben, your right, there is a boy with them wolves. And I thought I’d seen everything!” They stayed there just about all night trying to get in, but had no luck.

Doc and Ben just sat there drinking my grandpa’s homemade moonshine until they passed out. They both told the story over and over but everyone thought it just the moonshine talking. One night in March the town mayor was taking a walk along the flat wood paths and came back to town with his clothes just a hanging off him and ripped to pieces, like a pack of wolves had got a hold of him.

He told the same story Doc and Ben had told about a boy on his all fours. With a little checking, we found out about 17 years before that some people were camped out in the flat woods, and a one year old baby had crawled away from the camp and was never found. The men of town went back in the flat wood looking at day, (because no one would go in the dark of night) but with no luck. I bet he is still out there running with the wolves even to this day.

8

Burnt Ends

I woke up to the sun shining in my eyes. Mom had hung an old rug over the window in the front room, but all the holes dinnit do much to stop the sunlight coming in. I looked over to the floor at my cousin Junior who was still sleeping. He had stayed overnight with me, and we got to stay up into the wee hours.

I got up as quiet as I could and tip-e-toed into the kitchen. I saw the bucket of water that my brother Kenny had drawn from the town well before he went to work. Kenny had to get up before the sun so he could get his chores done before he went to work.

I got an idea, cold water would wake Junior up and it would be funny too. So I got a glass of water and tip-e-toed back to the front room and looked down at Junior sleeping on the floor. I thought to myself how can I do this. I could just throw it on his face, not funny enough. I could throw it on his pants, but he would be mad because he only had one pair of pants with him. Then I got it! I would put it in his hand, and go out and get a chicken feather from the chicken pen.

I put the water in his hand and I got up quiet and tip-e-toed out the front door. Thinking all the way to chicken pen that this is going to be so funny. I got the feather and ran to the front door, I quietly opened the door and tip-e-toed back into the house. I got on my knees in front of Junior's head and started moving the feather under his nose. He began moving his nose a little. I almost let out a big laugh, but I held my breath to stop it from coming out.

Just a couple more tickles I thought! So I twitched the feather under his nose again. He jerked the water in his hand, and threw it right in my face! As fast as it hit me in my face, he let out a big laugh.

"No fun!" I said, "No fun at all!"

"It was funny little Mac." He giggled, "Because your plan backfired on you!"

I looked at him with a loser look on my face and said "You was playing possum on me the whole time." He looked at me with a look of a winner on his face and said, "Yeps."

"It was a little bit fun." I said with a half smile across my face. I headed to the kitchen to get a rag to wash off my face. Junior followed right behind me talking about being hungry. I told him "You know we are not allowed to get into the food without asking Mom."

She was still sleeping. "Do you want to wake her up? because I know I don't!"

It was the weekend, the only two days she got to sleep in. We needed to find something to do, to take our minds off of eating. Junior looked at me with a half grin on his face. I knew that grin meant trouble for me, and in my house when you got in trouble, it was bad.

So I looked at him with a worried look on my face and asked, "What?"

He said "You know your brother Charles?"

I replied "Yes, I know Charles dummy, he is my brother."

Junior said "Well I saw him hide his smokes last night when he came home from his date." I knew he was telling the truth, because in my house if you get caught smoking, you were in for it. And it didn't matter how old you were.

Charles was 19 and he still knew better than to bring smokes into mom's house.

I said "Ok, so what?"

Junior said "There some matches in the kitchen and I know where some smokes is. Put two and two together little Mac!"

I thought to myself, I can count and it still adds up to trouble for me. I never tried the smokes before, so I let curiosity take over my good sense. I said "Ok! Let's go for it!" So we headed to the kitchen to get the matches. As soon as we got the matches, we tip-e-toed outside.

Junior followed me, and we went out to the back of the house. He said "Down there!" Pointing to the root cellar!

I said "Okay, but don't break any of my mom's can goods. We started down the dark stairs to the cellar door. We slowly opened the door and it was dark as night in there.

Junior lit a match so we could see our way. We got to the back of the cellar and he pointed up at an air pipe in the cellar roof. So I put up a bucket lying on the floor under the pipe. As Junior held the matches in his hand, I climbed up on the bucket and put my hand in the pipe.

As I felt around in the pipe, I thought about a snake taking a bite out of my hand, or maybe a spider. It only took a second and I felt the smokes. I grabbed them and said "Let's get the heck out of here!". So we got out of the cellar as fast as we could.

"Now, where can we go to hide and try one?" Junior asked.

I looked at him and said "The front porch!"

"A great place to hide, little Mac, a great place!" Junior said. So we ran out and got on our knees and crawled back under the porch. We got as far as we could go and stopped. Junior told me "I've tried smokes before, and since you haven't, you can go first.

"I'm only nine and you're only ten, so how could you have tried them before?" I asked.

"At school, big John made me! It was, try a smoke, or he was going to beat me up, so I tried the smoke.

I took one out of the pack and put it between my lips, it tasted bad.

Junior had the matches in his hands, he took one out and lit it. Junior told me, "Suck as hard as you can on the smoke as soon as I get the match to the end of the smoke, okay?"

I said "Okay!" And as soon as he got the match to the end of the smoke, I sucked super hard.

As I sucked on the cigarette, the flame from the match got bigger. It got so big it flared up and caught the ends of my hair on fire! I got so much of the smoke down my throat I began coughing and could not stop! Junior started patting my hair, trying to get the fire off.

By the time I stopped coughing and he got my hair put out, My hair was burnt so bad on the end! I began crying out "Oh no! Mom is gonna kill me, she is going to beat me till I'm dead!

Junior cried out "I've got an idea!"

I replied "Junior, your ideas got me in this condition in the first place!"

"Are you going listen to me or what?"

I said. "I guess I will, just because I've got none."

"Okay" he said. Let's go to the town well and draw some water." "We are not allowed at the well though, if we get caught, then we are gonna make the whole town mad at us!"

"I'm all ears if you can think of something we can do." Junior said.

"Okay." I replied. But I was scared we were going to get caught. We slowly crawled out from under the porch and made our way up the road to the well.

We looked around to see if anyone was in sight. Junior said "All the town folk are still sleeping!" So we walked up to the right side the well where the bucket was. As I slowly dropped the bucket into the well, Junior kept a lookout.

I dropped the bucket into the water and filled it full of water. Then I put the rope on the bucket till it was back to the top. I looked at Junior and said "Now what?"

He said "Put some water on your hands and wet your hair down with the water."

So I did as he said. "What now?" I asked.

He just reached into his back pocket and pulled out a comb. "Now comb your hair back." I did as he said.

"Let me see." Junior said.

"It looks great, no burnt ends Little Mac."

I asked "What about when it dries?"

"Little Mac, we can think on that when it happens." Junior replied.

By that time mom was calling out the back door, "Little Mac, Junior it's time to eat!" So we hurried back to my house. As we walked into the back door mom looked hard at my hair. "Hey little Mac, You are looking good! If you weren't my son I would give all the little girls around here a fight for you."

My brother Dave was sitting at the table, and I knew he wouldn't be quiet about me. So he said "He looks like a big geek!"

Mom told him to be quiet, and for us to go wash our hands. We did as we were told and by the time we got back, the whole family was sitting around the table.

So we took our seat, mom blessed the food, and we all started eating. In the middle of eating my hair was getting dry, and one piece at a time started falling down. I was not paying attention. Junior whispered in my ear, "Your hair!"

"Oh Mom, I need to go to the bathroom?" I blurted out.

On that she replied, "You can wait until we all get done eating."

By this time my hair had all fallen down. I thought maybe she wouldn't notice.

My brother Dave was looking at me so hard it was like he was looking right though me. "Hey Mom!" Dave said. "The little geek has burnt the end of his hair off!"

Mom looked right at me and jumped up from her chair! She ran around like the house was on fire. She got right up in my face and she started staring at my hair. She made me open my mouth so she could smell my breath, and my clothes. She said with a mad look on her face, "Boys get up and go out back and get me a switch!"

As we were leaving, Dave said "The little geek is in trouble now! Ha! Ha!"

Mom looked right at him and asked, "Do you need some too?"

"No." He replied.

So I get in the back yard looking for a switch. I knew it needed to be a thin one, and a long one. Because I had been here before, I'm not the new kid when it comes to picking a switch. We waited by the root cellar for her. I could tell Junior was scared about being switched. I knew its going to hurt, but just for a day or two.

We saw the back door come open, and Mom walked out. I could tell by the way she was walking she was really mad. "Where did you get the smokes from?"

I wanted to speak up first, because Junior would spill the beans about how we found them. And I knew my brother Charles would hurt me ten times more than Mom would!

"Where did you boys find them at?" She asked again.

Junior opened his mouth first. "The pack was over by the well, and I put them back where we found them."

I thought, 'Oh no, now we are in trouble for smoking, and being by the well! You big dummy!'

Mom looked at Junior and said, "Go get them now!" So he went.

"LITTLE MAC! Let us see, you're in trouble for playing with fire, smoking and for being by the well. Did I leave anything else out?" Mom asked.

"No Mom, you got everything." I said. Before dummy Junior could get back and think of something else. After a minute or so, Junior had made it back with the smokes and the matches, and gave them to her. "Oh!" she said. "You took my matches from the kitchen! Something else I can add to the list."

"Alright little Mac, push your pant legs up." Mom said. So I did as I was told and she lay into my legs with the switch. It felt like fire burning me every time that switch hit my legs! She didn't even stop till blood was coming out of both legs. Junior was watching and was just shaking like a leaf on a tree.

She got done with me and looked at Junior, and he begin pushing his pant legs up.

She looked at him and said, "No, I'm not your Mom. Now you go in the house, and tell Otis to take you home and tell your Mom and Dad what you have done. Oh, and Junior I'll ask them if you left anything out.

Junior said as he took off, "I'll see you at school on Monday little Mac."

With that he was gone. She turned back to me and saw that the blood was getting my pant leg wet. "Here Little Mac, now sit down and eat this whole pack of smokes. ALL of them!"

I ate the whole pack of smokes, and threw up about ten times. Mom said "Alright little Mac, go in the house and put some medicine On the back of our legs. You're grounded for the whole weekend."

So that's the story of the burnt ends, and I never smoked again.

9

The Boy

With a Girl's Name

It was a cold afternoon in November of 1953, on Thanksgiving Day. An older lady impatiently paced the floor, while in the other room her daughter lay in bed in pain. The older lady is going to be my Grandma, and the lady in the other room is going to be my Mom, as soon as she gives birth today.

I'm Little Mac. Well I will be! Grandma let out a bad word, and said "Where is that man of yours? I'll bet he's behind the feed store in Leeper throwing dice and losing all his money! He needs to be here with you, you're having his kid!"

Mom replied "He will be here, I'm sure of it!"

Grandma was not going to wait, she opened the door and hollered out at my brother to get going to Leeper. And on the way, to stop and tell Dr. Pithy to get down here. "Your mother is laying here in pain, and she's getting really close. Then go behind the feed store, and tell your no-good daddy to get home right now!"

Kenny said, "Yes ma'am, I'm leaving right now!"

Mom said, "Don't ever let me hear you talk about their dad like that in front of the kids."

Grandma turned her head, and talked into her hands, "It's the truth, and the truth hurts!"

Then Grandma lifted her head from her hands. "You just watch and see, your man will come home drunk and broke! I'll bet my bottom dollar on that! Here you are with four kids and one on the way today, and he isn't even here!"

Mom was getting mad at her ma and dad both. So she said "Where's your man at, out with my man getting drunk too?"

Grandma said, "I'm not having a baby!"

Mom said, "No you have already had 15 kids, and he was out drunk on all of them I bet!"

It was just about a half an hour later when Dr. Pithy pulled up in his horse and buggy. He got a black bag from the back of the buggy and came through the front door. He asked, "How far apart are the contractions?"

Grandma replied, "About five minutes!"

Dr. Pithy told her, "Boil some water on the stove!"

Grandma told him, "Are you talking to me? if so, you better take that tone out of your voice right now, before I knock it out!"

Dr. Pithy asked again, "Would you please boil some water, Mrs. Laxton?"

She said, "Yes I will!"

Dr. Pithy went into the bedroom to check on me and Mom. "How are you doing Mrs. McFadden?"

She said, "I'm ready to get this baby out of me!"

At that time, my sister Kathy who was three and a half years old, turned over in the other bed and woke up crying."

"Mrs. Laxton would you take the baby in the front room please?" Dr. Pithy said to my Grandma.

Grandma came in from the kitchen, picked up Kathy and walked back out of the room without saying a word.

It was around 6:00 pm. When I was birthed, a little baby boy. Doc cleaned me up, give me to my Mom, and said, "A big boy, 8 pounds and 2 ounces."

Afterward, he pulled some paperwork out of his black bag. He asked Mom "What is this little boy going to go by?" Now Dr. Pithy was just a little hard of hearing, so that oughta explain what happened next. Mom said "His name is going to be Norman Bruce."

Doc said "Alright!" Thinking to his self, 'What a crazy name for a boy!" He turned to his paperwork and wrote the name Norma Bruce McFadden. He then turned back to my Mom and said, "If you need anything send one of the kids to get me. I'm going to be at the Johnson farm. One of the cows are going to have a baby sometime tonight."

See Dr. Pithy isn't a real Doctor at all, he is a veterinarian. But he is the closest thing to a Doctor that we had for miles.

It was about midnight when my finally Dad came in, about as quietly as a tree falling on the house! Just like Grandma said, he was drunk and broke.

I was the only turkey the McFadden family got that Thanksgiving, Nov. 22nd, 1953. An 8 pound 2 ounce boy, with a girl's name.

Note from the Author: This story was told by Little Mac's Grandmother. It is also noted that, shortly after Little Mac's birth, his Father's behavior changed greatly. He became a man well-liked and respected within the community, and was no longer known to drink or gamble. And while Little Mac's family was poor, in the sense that they had no money, they were very rich in the love they had from their Mom and Dad.

10

Bum's Cave

It's a beautiful day in the Spring of nineteen and thirty five. The sun is shining down on a small hill near the town of Mill Spring, Missouri. The flowers are blessing the hillside with beauty, the birds are singing theirs song of love. New life was blooming everywhere.

In this little town, everything is right with the world.

Mr. Johnson was opening his little store, where he sold everything from horseshoes and hay bales, to milk and eggs. He had just walked to the back of the store to open up the side door. Some folks liked using the side door for some reason. The first to walk into the store was Ray and Eric. There were two old men who sat at the back of the store playing checkers all day.

They had been there about an hour when Sheriff Thomson came in. It just so happened that Tom came in a minute later with something in his arms. Following right behind him was his only friend in the world, Billy. Billy was calling out to the Sheriff, “It’s your niece, Sue!”

Sue was his brother’s little girl, and she was only ten years old. The Sheriff met him half way, and took little Sue from Tom’s arms. He ran to the back of the store where the old men were playing checkers. Mr. Johnson threw the checker board to the floor as the Sheriff lay little Sue on the table.

The Sheriff looked at Tom and Billy and said, “You two don’t go anywhere. I’m going to get the Doctor. When I get back, you two got some questions to answer!”

Mr. Johnson did what he could to help little Sue, but he thought it was too late by the looks of it. He was afraid that she was already gone.

It took the sheriff about a half an hour to get back with the Doctor. As they came into the store, he told Ray to go and find Sue’s dad. He looked at Tom and Billy and said, “You two come with me.” He took them out to the front part of the store to talk with them.

“Tell me what happened.” Said the Sheriff. “And start talking now!”

Tom spoke up. “Me and Billy was walking down the railroad tracks, and happened to look over by the spring. We saw one of them crazy hobos bending over little Sue. We hollered out, ‘Hey you! what are you doing?’.”

He looked up at us on the tracks, then he picked up a big rock and hit her right in the head with it. We ran down as fast as we could. By the time we got there, he was gone. Little Sue was lying on the grass with her pants down around her feet. I pulled them up and got her here as fast as I could.

The Sheriff, with a suspicious look on his face, asked Billy,

“Have you got anything to add?”

Tom said, “He hasn’t got anything to add sheriff.”

“I would like to hear that from Billy!” Said the Sheriff.

“It happened just like Tom said.” Replied Billy. He would never go against Tom on anything, because he knew what Tom was capable of doing to him.

About that time Sue’s dad, Jimmy, came in. “Where is my baby girl at Sheriff?”

“She’s with the Doctor in back.” The Sheriff told him.

“How is she?” Jimmy asked. “Go back and ask the doctor.” said the Sheriff.

So Jimmy rushed to the back of the store. The Doctor looked at him and shook his head. Then he covered up Sue's face and turned to say, "Sorry, but she is gone."

Jimmy lay across her, crying, and said, "She was only ten, just a baby!"

The Doctor spoke to the sheriff, and said, "She was raped before she was killed."

Her dad Jimmy overheard what the doctor said. "Who found her?" He asked.

Tom said, "I did, and I saw who done it to her. It was one of those hobos from down at bums cave!"

*-**BACKSTORY**: In the 1930's it was hard times for all, but for some it was harder. Men would leave their families and travel from town to town looking for work. They was called hobos and would stay in the cave right along the railroad tracks. It was home to as many as 20 hobos sometimes. But never the same ones. It was easy to get off and on the train, because it stops at a little station in the nearby town of Mill Spring.*

Tom said, “Let’s go down there and kill them all! Right now! They all just bums, who would care if we kill them all? We will get the right one!”

Jimmy said, “Okay, I’ll go home and get my gun. Tom you get some rope and we will meet at the train station. We’re gonna take care of all our problems at the same time!”

The Sheriff said, “I can’t let you all do that!”

Jimmy grabbed his brother by the hand and pulled him back to where Sue was laid on the table. He pulled the cover from her little body. “Take a look brother, that was your beautiful niece! Now look at her face so beaten and bloody that you can hardly recognize her. She was only ten, and they raped her!”

The Sheriff looked up with a sad look on his face, and said, “I’m going to go out of town on a fishing trip, so do what you must. I won’t be around to help you, or stop you.” After that he walked out of the store, got in his car, and left.

It took about two hours for the men to meet at the train station. The sun was high in the sky. It was sometime around noon. Tom and Billy were the first to get there. Mr. Johnson came, and brought his gun with him. He had closed his store to take part in it. Ray and Eric had both gone home and got their guns, and joined the rest. They all started down the tracks to the cave.

Billy stopped to speak his mind. “Maybe we shouldn’t do this Tom.”

Tom pulled him to the side and told him, “If you don’t start walking the track, I’ll shoot you, tie your legs and throw you in the river!” With that Billy did not say another word. They kept on walking down the tracks.

Soon they arrived in the area of the cave. But when the men ran up the hill to the cave, Billy stayed on the tracks, looking at the Black River rolling down toward the south. He heard the gun shots, and could smell the gunpowder in the air. He never moved. He heard the cry from the hobos, and the shouting of the men at the hobos.

He looked up from the river, and could see an old black man coming down the hill from the cave. Tom was right behind him calling out, “Billy get him, he’s getting away!”

But the old man stopped and fell at Billy’s feet. “Help me, I didn’t do anything!”

Billy looked him in the eyes and said, “I know you didn’t.” By that time Tom got there and put his gun to the back of the old man’s head. When he shot him, the blood splattered on Billy face. Billy just stood there and watched as the town men dragged all the hobos to the river. They tied weights onto their legs, and threw them all into the river. After that, they all walked back the way they came. Billy sat there all day and watched the river roll on by.

It was two months later when Billy accidentally shot Tom on a hunting trip. Tom died. Two months after that, the sheriff got drowned on a fishing trip. Three months later, Ray was found hanging in his barn. Two days later Eric choked to death on a chicken bone. Mr. Johnson, a month latter, was shot by a robber who came in through the side door that some of the folks liked to use. Jimmy, Sue's dad knew it wasn't right that all those men were killed. He just ended up putting a gun to his head and took his own life.

It was three years to the day after the massacre, that someone found a letter nailed to a tree. It was beside the river where the fifteen hobos had met their end. This is what the letter said: '*I Billy, need for all you to know the truth. I and Tom were walking down the train tracks and saw Sue picking flowers along the spring. He said look at Little Sue, she's growing up fast. I think I'll go down and get a kiss from her.*

So we walked down to talk to her, and Tom started hurting her. She tried to run away. Tom got her and pulled her to the ground, then he raped her. That's when a hobo from up on the tracks saw us and hollered at us. Before I knew what was happening, Tom had picked up a rock and hit her in the head two or three times. He got up and hit me, and I fell to the ground. He got on top of me and said 'If you tell anybody about what happened here I'll cave your head in with a rock!'

I knew that he would too, so I kept my mouth shut! It was all over, I had to kill every man who took part in the hobos killing but one. That is me. I'm going to tie a rock onto my legs, fall into the river and let it roll me south.'

They say, at noon, by the Black River along the train tracks, on the patch going up the hill to a lonely cave, You can still hear the cry of the hobos. You can sometimes hear the shots of the guns, and still smell the gunpowder in the air.

11

The Day the World Cried

It was November 21st of 1963. A chilly rain was falling on a Thursday evening. The old King heater was blazing red hot! I was sitting as close as I could get to the wood heater, as the cold winds of an early winter blew through the side boards of our small, southern Missouri home. Nestled in the hills of Leeper.

My name is Little Mac. I am all excited because tomorrow is my birthday. They are even gonna throw me a party at the school! With it being so cold outside, I've been hiding inside and trying to keep away from David, my brother. He seems to get his enjoyment out of beating me up.

I had been working with Mom, I helped her set the table for supper. She had a smile on her face as if to say

"Thank you Little Mac!" And then she said "You had better go and get washed up while I call in the other kids." So I went to the wash basin and got cleaned up.

I hurried up and got seated at the table before David came in. I knew he wouldn't hurt me too bad in front of Mom. Well, mention the Devil and here he comes. As he walked by to sit down, he smacked me on the back of my head and said "How you doing little brother? You got real lucky today, lets see if your luck holds out tomorrow!" Mom had an angry look on her face. My brother seemed to have that affect on people.

Mom said to David "Young man, what do you mean by that?"

He knew not to cross Mom. She was a small lady but he knew that dynamite comes in small packages! David said "Oh nothing, Mom, I love my little brother, he is my world!" I thought to myself, 'Liar!'

When we got done eating, Mom told us, "It's time for bed, you all have school tomorrow."

So after we finished up our supper, it was off to bed we went. I was almost always nervous come bedtime. I never knew what to expect, because I had to sleep with my brother David.

Most of the time, I would be sleeping with one eye open all night. Hopefully, everything would be alright tonight. To fall asleep at night, I would often think of the beautiful woods that God had created. It was a peaceful place to escape, even if only in my head. And I was able to fall asleep.

After I woke up the next morning, I was sure glad to see that David was still asleep. I hurried up to get my chores done before he could wake up. I sure didn't want him to catch me outside. After I finished them up, I helped Mom in the kitchen while the other kids did their chores.

So I helped Mom set the table, we all sat down and ate breakfast. All I could think about was getting to school for my birthday party at one o'clock! You see, being poor in the nineteen sixties, presents and birthday parties were very special. Simple things like food on the table, shoes on your feet and clothes on your back were the first priority. And not even those things were always possible. So this was going to be a very cool day!

As I grabbed my lunch bag to head out the door and beat David to the bus stop, Mom grabbed me. "Say little Mac, I think I'm going to drive you to school today!"

David whined, "Not fair!" I think that she knew I was afraid to be at the bus stop with him. And she didn't do this very often.

I guess it was a special day for me after all. And so after my brothers and sisters left for the bus stop, I sat on the couch and waited for Mom to get ready. After sitting there, and sitting there, she finally came in from the other room with her purse in her hand.

She smiled at me, "I'm ready little Mac."

So I ran out and jumped into the front seat of the car. She got in and said, “Happy birthday son!”

On the way to school we stopped by the station for some gas. Mom whispered, “I have a surprise for you little Mac.”

I said, “Well you better hurry up, Mom, It’s getting late and my party starts at one o’clock!”

She looked at me with a warm smile, “Son, I will get you there on time. I just wanted to spend a little time with you and talk to you about something.”

And so she started the car, with a clunk from the engine and a puff of black smoke we were off. Another reality of being so poor, always driving junk cars that sound like they are going to blow up at any moment! But it got us where we needed to go, and I was just anxious to get there as quickly as we could!

We finally got to Judge Lucy’s General Store and Mom pulled out a nickel before we opened our doors.

“Here you go little Mac, get you an ice cream or some candy, whatever you want. It’s your special day!” Then she handed me a whole dollar and said, “Tell Judge Lucy I’m getting a dollar’s worth of gas.”

I went in and began to look around for some goodies. I saw some penny candy and thought to myself, ‘If I buy some of that, I will have candy all day long!’, so I got my candy and went to the register.

"Why aren't you in school today little Mac?" Asked the Judge.

"I'm on my way to school right now. They are throwing me a birthday party today!"

"It's your birthday today little Mac?" I nodded happily. "In that case, you can go and pick out two more pieces of candy. And happy birthday from the general store!"

I picked out the candy, stuffed it into my bag and out the door I ran! Mom had already pumped the gas and was waiting for me in the car.

"Get in little Mac, I'm going to take you somewhere special so we can have a talk." We left the general store and crossed the railroad tracks. We drove on past the feed store, and then the baseball field and parked down at the mill pond. By this time, it was getting close to noon. I was getting very anxious about being late for my own party!

She looked at me and reached for my hand. "Little Mac, I just wanted to tell you that when you come home from school tonight, me and your Dad won't be there. But don't you worry, we will have someone there to watch you while we are gone."

I didn't understand what was going on. They were always there. "No! Not David! It's not David is it!?"

"No, it's not David. He is going to be with us. Now give me a piece of that candy little Mac and I will drop you off at the school."

So we headed to the school. I made it before the party! And with a little time to spare. I got out of the car and watched her leave with a large cloud of smoke.

As I walked into the school, I could tell that something was very wrong. There were several students in the hallway just sobbing and crying. Teachers were holding tissues to their eyes and the Principal was running around like a chicken with it's head cut off!

I walked into my classroom thinking "Was everyone sad because it was my birthday!?"

My teacher was also crying, and so were the students in my class! I sat down at my desk. My best friend Jimmy was sitting next to my desk. And he wasn't crying at all. So I asked him, "What's going on?"

"Oh, some rich man bit the bullet today." He shrugged at me.

"Who was it?" I asked him quietly.

"Our President, John F. Kennedy got shot. I don't know if he's alive or dead."

It wasn't too long before our Principal came in the classroom and announced that the President was dead. Everyone began to cry all the louder! Everyone but me and Jimmy that is.

And this was announced just before we were supposed to have my party! And now it was canceled. No party, no presents for little Mac. If anybody should have been crying, it was me! And if that wasn't lousy enough for my birthday, I found out when I got home, that my sister Kathy was gonna be babysitting me. And she's only two and a half years older than me. Well, on the bright side, at least Mom and Dad had taken David with them. That boy is the seed of Satan! And he did everything in his power to make my life miserable.

Still, I was wondering what they were going out for? 'Maybe to get me a present!' I thought. Me and Kathy just sat around playing some games. We started a game of checkers, but I knew it would probably turn out like usual. I would win, then she would get mad and throw the checkerboard across the room. I would always win at checkers. It was like a gift from God!

I will say this though, she was a challenge for me sometimes. But not today! I could see her face getting redder and redder as I was closing in on the win! She made me think of a tea kettle on top of a wood stove as it got hotter and hotter. You could watch the steam coming out, step back, she's about to blow!

She fell right into my trap, with a triple jump to seal the deal, it was all over. 'Here we go again!' I thought to myself. She jumped up, slammed her chair and started screaming at me.

"You pea brain little dirt bag! I ain't talking to you anymore!"

She picked up the checkerboard and dumped all the pieces onto the floor. But this time, instead of throwing the board across the room, she firmly gripped it, and whacked me upside the head with it! Then she called me a few choice words that I won't mention in a family book. And then she stomped away to her room.

As I was cleaning up the mess, I heard a car pull up in the drive. It was Mom and Dad back with my present! I heard Dad yell at David to stop slamming the door. And it sounded like someone was crying too. I looked out the window to see. It was Mom crying. Dad had his arm around her to comfort her.

'Was she crying because they couldn't afford a present for me? I will say something nice to cheer her up when they walk in the door.' I thought to myself. The door opened and I ran over to them as they walked in.

"Heck, don't worry about not getting me a present! I don't give a doggone about no presents anyway. My family is what's most important me, as long as we're all together that is better than any present."

David had a real mean look on his face and told me, "That's the biggest load of crap I ever heard, little Mac! You are so full of crap it's coming out your ears! You always have to make it about you. Get over yourself!"

Mom screamed at him, "If I wasn't so upset I would wash your mouth out with soap, boy! You go to your room now and think about what you've done!" I thought to myself, 'Yeah, he's gonna think alright. Think about how to kill me!'

As David was walking by to go to his room, he stared at me with that evil look in his eyes, and I knew I was right. "Little Mac, I'm gonna give you your birthday present later, but you are not going to like it!"

I knew exactly what he meant by that. And I'm sure he was right, I wasn't going to like it one bit! It was an old tradition.

You get spanked for every year and a pinch to grow on. But for David, it was just another excuse to beat me up. And when he spanked it was real hard, and his pinches were worse than when he shot me in the butt with a b.b gun. And that was pretty bad, because Mom had to pick it out with the tweezers!

It was so sad to see my Mom crying. She was like an angel sent down from God. She took such good care of us. She was always the first one up, and the last one to go to bed. She worked hard, and even had the calloused hands to prove it. She took me by the hand and set me down on the couch.

"Little Mac, we didn't get your present. We found out that our beloved President was shot and killed today. And that's why I am so sad."

I just didn't understand why she was so sad. It was just another rich man that didn't give a hill of beans about us poor people. We were so poor we didn't even have indoor plumbing. In the Winter, the cold wind would blow the snow through the cracks in the wall and freeze a glass of water and break it!

We were so poor, we only got new shoes once a year. And if they wore out, we would have to stuff some cardboard in them. And I didn't even own a pair of socks! So how could some rich man ever understand what it was like to be so poor? Maybe I just couldn't understand at the young age of ten.

"What did he ever do for us?" I asked her.

A smile came across her face, "He was a good man. He helped people who couldn't afford to eat. Even people here in Leeper get help from the government little Mac."

She was talking about welfare. My Dad said that wasn't for us. He said a man should earn his living by the sweat of his brow. He was a proud man. And he told me to never cry in front of anyone. He said men don't cry in public. If I had to cry, to go and do it in private. I believed that for many years.

After my Grandpa's funeral, my cousin thought I didn't care for him because I didn't cry. I loved Grandpa so much and bawled my eyes out after I got home. I learned it's alright to show emotion in front of others that day.

So after talking with Mom, I went over to Jimmy's house to play. When I got there his Mom opened the door. She was crying too. As I walked through the house, I saw his sisters crying like babies also. I came to his room and pulled the curtain back. He didn't have a door for his room. I heard that his Dad had ripped it off the hinges one night when he was mad.

Thank God, He wasn't crying! Someone that actually wasn't crying on my birthday! He was playing with an old beat up toy truck that only had two of it's wheels left on it.

"Thank you Jimmy!" I said.

He asked me, "Thanks for what?"

"For not crying over President Kennedy!"

Now Jimmy was colder than I was. He didn't care at all for rich people. He had it worse than even I. His Dad was a drunkard. He would come in from a night of drinking and beat Jimmy up. He would beat up Jimmy's Mom too. Years later after they moved away, I heard Jimmy killed his Dad for beating up his Mom. They said he was serving life in prison. It was sad. But it helped me to realize that it's not about what happens to you in life, but what you do with it that counts.

So I asked Jimmy, "You wanna go out to our hideout, to get away from all this crying?

He answered, "Okay, little Mac, but first I have a present for you."

'A present? I am actually gonna get a present on my birthday!' I thought. He pulled something out from under his mattress. It was a flat rock with paper eyes and legs glued on it. It wouldn't mean much to most kids, but to me it meant the world! He had made it with his heart. It wasn't something you could just go out and buy at a store.

I kept that present from him until I lost everything in a house fire at the age of 26. So we went out to our hideout. The one place where it didn't matter if you were rich or poor. It was God's beautiful creation out there in the woods. We were safe from taking a beating. Whether it was from my brother David, or Jimmy getting one from his Dad.

Our hideout was made of limbs we put in the ground, covered with clay and added more limbs. We talked and enjoyed each other's company until dark.

As the light was fading, we knew that our escape from reality was over. It was time to go back to the life that we did not choose. On that cold and rainy November day, that the world cried, we said goodbye and headed home. Unsure of what the next day would bring.

Shortly after that, he moved away and I never saw him again. But nothing can take away the memories that I have.

Today, I understand what a ten year old boy could not grasp on his birthday. The President was more than just a man. He was the hope for a nation. And that hope was taken away with a bullet.

In Loving Memory of

John F. Kennedy

May 29, 1917 – November 22, 1963

What were you doing that day?

12

Grandma Brown's Ghost

It was 1961 and school was out for the Summer. I'm little Mac, a seven year old boy that wants nothing more than to go outside and play. But it's been raining cats and dogs all day long! I had my knees dug in to the couch with my face in my hands, imagining that angels were pouring buckets of water from the sky above. I just sat there looking out the window at the rain. I would even occasionally sing a little song.

"Rain, rain, go away, come again another day. Little Mac wants to go out and play!" There is not much else to do. Just try to keep away from my brother David. But in a four room house, it's really hard to hide from someone that wants to kill you!

Mom was in the Kitchen getting ready to fry up some chicken for lunch. My sister Kathy was playing with her paper dolls. She had cut them out of some old Sears catalogs we kept in the outhouse. That thing was terrible! Hot in the summer, freezing in the winter. And there would be wasp nests in it all the time. I can't remember how many times I was stung just trying to go to the bathroom. And those old catalogs and newspapers, that's what we had to use out there. We didn't have the fancy toilet paper.

My Dad had left with Mr. Fisher to see if they could make some money hauling stuff with Mr. Fisher's truck. My brothers Charles and Kenny were out riding.

Mom came into the living room from the kitchen and yelled, "Kids, I want you all in here now!"

Kathy and David came running in, Mom told them, "Sit there on the couch next to little Mac!"

I thought to myself, 'Oh great, David is gonna be pinching me now!'

She said, "I'm going to tell you all a story."

Alright! I love stories, I will listen to anyone's stories!

As she began to speak, the thunder was rolling outside. She said, "I'm going to tell you the story of Grandma Brown's ghost!" Just as she said that, lightning struck an electric pole and the lights went out! She got a flashlight and shined it on her face. David and Kathy huddled up real close to me on the couch.

She continued, "It happened during my first pregnancy. I was only 15 years old. And your Dad was 21. He was still a little wild, there were many nights he stayed out drinking all night and I was home alone. As a pregnant 15 year old, I would walk to my Mom and Dad's house to stay the night when he didn't come home.

"We were living in an old box car that the railroad company had left in a field. There were three of them together that made up different rooms. No water, no electric. It was hot in the summer and cold in the Winter. We didn't have no money, so that was the best we could do.

"Now Grandma Brown lived with my Mom and Dad. I would stay over there when your Dad was at work in the daytime. So between the work day and being out drinking all night, I spent a lot of time over there.

"Grandma Brown was old and sick. She didn't get up and around much, but when she did, you sure knew it. She walked with a cane that had soda caps nailed to the bottom of it. So whenever she would walk across the floor, her cane made a click, click, click sound.

"One night when I was about seven months into the pregnancy, I was sleeping over at Mom and Dad's. I awoke to a light on. Grandma Brown was standing over me. She touched my stomach and said, 'Baby I gotta go away, but I will come back to see you.'

"Then she turned away and I heard her cane on the floor as she left the room, click, click, click. I looked over at the clock to see that it was four in the morning! I though maybe it was just a dream, and fell back asleep.

"Later that morning, My Mom woke me up by running into the room crying. She calmed down a bit, then said that she had something to tell me. She said that sometime in the night, Grandma had died in her sleep! And what was really strange, was that her cane was missing. It was not beside her bed, where she had always kept it. It was like she had gone for a walk and hid it somewhere before she passed.

"Just then there was a knock on the door. It was your Dad. He was mad about me being over at Mom and Dad's again. But my Mom put him in his place real quick like. She said he had better get some electric on over there at our place, or else when the baby got here they were gonna take us away!

"She even made mention of her old double barrel shotgun a time or two! He started saying 'Yes Ma'am' and 'No Ma'am'! She told him that Grandma had just died so I was gonna stay there at home for the day. She said he should just go on home and get some sleep.

"We sat around most of the day and Mom told me stories about Grandma Brown. I went on home around four in the afternoon. A few weeks later, your Dad got us some electric hooked up. He even got a baby crib and put up a light above it! I think that talk my Mom had with him did a lot of good!

"About a month and a half later, your big brother Charles was born. It was around three weeks after he was born that it happened. We put him in his crib at 8 p.m. and me and your Dad went to bed. I was falling asleep right about ten o'clock, as I usually did when suddenly, I heard it.

"It was the unmistakable sound of Grandma Brown's cane going across the floor. Click, click, click. I jumped up and ran to where the noise was coming from. But there wasn't anything there. I lay back down and heard it again.

"I looked into the Baby's room and the light above his crib was on! But still, there wasn't anything there. I shut the light out and went back to bed, after a little time I fell asleep. The next morning, I was shocked when I went into his room. I saw the strangest thing ever… GRANDMA BROWN'S CANE WAS HANGING ON THE CRIB!!! She came back from the grave to visit her Great Grandson and even left him a present!

Norman Mcfadden

In loving memory of my brother

Charles E. Mcfadden

March 5th, 1944 – November 13th, 2015

And Grandmother

Lydia A. Laxton

January 16th, 1894 – April 12th, 1982

13

Vision of Hell

It is November 20th of 1965. I'm Little Mac and I live in a small backwoods town in southern Missouri, called Leeper. It's going to be my birthday in two days, I'm going to be twelve! It's about six p.m. and my brother's friend, Little Boy, is here, and he is trying to get my dad to go spotlighting for deer in the Nipper Woods.

"Not tonight, I'm not feelin' so well." My dad told him.

"That's cool." Little Boy said as he headed for the door, "I'll find something else to do." You could hear the disappointment in his voice as he went outside and let the door slam behind him.

Now let me tell you about Little Boy. He was my brother's best friend, but he was also our cousin. They were perfect together, just like two peas in a pod.

But I, in my young age thought that I was a preacher. I'd preach at anyone, at any time, especially if they would listen to me. But I would also preach at people who didn't want to hear it as well. It didn't matter to me who I was preaching to, I would keep on anyway.

Little boy fell into the second category, he certainly did not want to hear me preaching. I had learned before from preaching to him, but tonight I could feel something pushing me to go after him. And I knew to never fight the Spirit of God. So out the door I went, right behind him.

"Hey, Little Boy." I hollered to stop him. "It's my birthday in two days."

He bent down and smiled as he patted me on the head. "Well, happy almost-birthday Little Mac."

I smiled back at him, "You know what would make it a really good birthday?" I asked him.

"No." He said as he shook his head.

"If you would go to church with me and Mom."

"I don't need all that stuff, Little Mac." He chuckled a little. "I'm gonna have fun, partying here on earth with my friends. And then when I die and go to hell, I am gonna party with all my friends some more."

I looked at him and told him sternly. “There ain’t gonna be no partying in Hell! Nothing but suffering and sadness and fire, plain and simple.”

As Little Boy looked at me a sort of terrified look crossed his face. “Someone come back and tell you this Little Mac?”

“No.” I told him.

“Then you don’t really know what forever is like.” He told me.

As I looked at Little Boy an inner peace flooded through me, forcing a smile to come across my face. “No, no one came back and told me, but the Bible tells me that it’s so.”

He just laughed at me. “My little buddy.” He turned and walked away slowly.

As I watched his figure slowly disappear into the darkness I had a funny feeling deep down inside me. Something told me that this might be the last time that I ever saw Little Boy. I had to try again, I had to get him to come to church with us.

I ran down the road after him, finally catching him about halfway to his house. “Hey,” I caught his attention, “Please consider going to church with us, It really would make a great birthday present for me.”

As he turned to me he looked sad. “Alright, Little Mac, if it means that much to you then I’ll consider it.’ And with that he turned and was back on his way.

That night it was so hard for me to get to sleep. Somewhere around midnight I finally dropped off. Not too much later I was suddenly woke by a bright light in my eyes. I could see it was coming in through the window.

As I looked into the light there seemed to be something in the center of it. It came closer and closer. Before long I could see that it was a person.

This person floated right through my window and hovered over my bed. I was so terrified! I couldn't even move. As I watched it I realized that the person was Little Boy, he was floating right over top of me.

He reached out his hand for me, I was perfectly still, too scared to move.

"Take his hand." A voice from nowhere spoke to me.

I was so scared, but I did what the voice said. For just a moment we floated above my bed, hand in hand. Then out the closed window we went, like a ghost, without even busting the glass.

We went high up into the sky. As I looked down on the Earth it looked different. I soon started hearing the sounds of people crying out in pain. It was a horrible sound, and it seemed to come from everywhere at once.

I looked as we came closer and could see single holes in the ground. There were millions of them, as far as the eye could see. Out of every hole came the putrid odor of decaying, burning flesh. My nose and eyes started to burn from the smell, and tears ran down my cheeks.

Closer still and I could see the flames in the holes, sometimes shooting up into the sky. We were about thirty feet up now and I could feel the heat of the flames, it was just so hot.

We kept getting closer to the ground as we flew over hole after hole for what seemed like hours. We were close enough now that I could see human figures moving around in the holes.

On and on we flew until finally stopping above a single one. It was about ten feet across and close to twenty feet deep. Little Boy wouldn't let go of me, he pulled me closer and closer.

"I don't want to go in there! Please, please! Take me home!" I cried out in terror.

He said nothing, not a single word. He just kept lowering me toward that hole. As we came nearer the flames seemed to part for us.

I thought I would try again. "Please, take me home! I don't want to be here." I begged, I plead for mercy. But he didn't respond.

I could feel the heat and the flames all around me now.

"God forgive me. I knew not what I was doing." A voice cried out from somewhere in the pit below me.

We were about halfway down into the hole and the heat was so intense that I thought my face was melting. I looked down below me and could clearly see the person who had cried out. It was my cousin, Little Boy, standing there all alone.

Just then the spirit that had been holding me let go of my hand and disappeared. Slowly I began to fall, lower and lower. My body felt like it was melting. I knew that it was too hot, that I was going to die.

"Lord help me, please. I am going to die." I said to God. Somehow, though, I didn't die.

About six feet above where Little Boy stood I stopped falling and seemed to float in the air.

He looked up at me with tears flowing down his face. "You were right, I'm not partying with my friends. I'm alone in this pit for all eternity to burn and burn and burn, and never die."

I could feel myself beginning to fall again, right before I hit the ground I was suddenly woke by someone knocking hard at our front door. I looked around me and saw my bedroom, I was still in my bed!

"Thank you, Lord." I looked toward heaven and said.

I could hear my dad say a few curse words as he thumped out of his own bed. "Who in the sam-hill is at my front door, at this time of night?"

I got up and followed him to the door. It was our neighbor, Clyde. "Come right now!" He said to my dad.

"Not 'til I know what in the sam-hill is going on." My dad told him.

"There's been a terrible wreck down at the end of the holler, on the highway." Clyde told him.

"Alright, let me stick some clothes on." My dad said as he headed back to his room to get dressed.

As my dad was dressing, I ran to get dressed too!

"Let's go." My dad said as he came back in the living room pulling on his shirt

They headed down the road about as fast as they could run. I followed behind, but stayed back a little ways, because I knew if they saw me that I'd be run back home. It was about a half mile to the end of the holler where the highway began.

Now in case you don't know what a holler is, let me tell you. It's a valley that sits between two large hills. Where the highway ends there is a gravel road that runs about two miles back into the valley, then dead ends.

"Hurry up." Clyde shouted to my dad as they ran on.

The highway here is very straight, but has a sudden sharp curve that has caught many drivers by surprise and sent them into the ditch.

"It's two of our boys from right here in the holler. One of 'em is still inside and the other was thrown through the windshield and hit the blacktop.

"Slow down and take me to them." Dad told Clyde.

As I came up to the wreck my senses were overwhelmed. I could see the skid marks where they had tried to brake before the car had run off the road and up a little hill where it hit a tree. Then rolled over onto it's top trapping the one boy inside. They were clearly going way too fast for the curve in the road.

I looked up the road to the other boy laying face down on the blacktop, blood running from his body and into the ditch. Broken glass around him and no less than six beer bottles next to the car.

I became overwhelmed by the smell of burning oil from the motor. Blood and liquor odors mixed in the air. Loud rock music was still coming from the car radio.

The boy inside the car began to cry for help as the wind whistled through the trees above the car. My dad and Clyde grunting and fighting the car to get the boy out.

They were so busy that they never saw me standing there seeing, hearing and smelling things that a twelve year old should never have to experience.

Finally they got him free from the car and carried him over and laid the boy in the grass. I was shocked to see that it was a boy I knew named Ronnie! He was pretty bruised up, but otherwise he looked okay.

Then they ran up the boy on the road. He lay about ten feet in front of the car. As they turned him over I sneaked closer, I wanted to see who it was. I could hardly recognize his face, it was so mangled from sliding up the blacktop. As I came closer I realized it was my eighteen year old cousin, my brother's best friend, Little Boy.

My head was filled with the vision that I had seen earlier that night. The vision of Hell!

In loving memory

Eugene McFadden

June 26, 1947-Nov 20, 1965

14

The Rooster That Should Have Died

It's a cold Friday, December 16th, 1960. The snow is gently falling and the ground has about four inches or so on it. Dad was out at the chicken coop this morning getting some eggs for breakfast. He came through the back door as mad as a wet hen. He was hollering "Those doggone foxes been eating up our chickens! They got two more last night!"

Mom took the eggs from Dad and he went into the other room to wash up. He came back and sat down at the table with us kids.

"I'm going to be thinking on it at work today. I'll come up with something to stop the foxes!" He muttered.

Mom just looked at him. You could see that there was some doubt in her eyes.

After she had scrambled up the morning eggs, she sat down at the table and said grace. She told us that she wasn't very hungry and she didn't eat. There were many times that she had done that. I now know that it was because there simply wasn't enough for everyone. And she wanted to make sure that we were all well fed. We didn't appreciate all of the sacrifices that she made for us. I have to take a moment now just to say, "Thanks Mom for all that you did for us!"

Dad took off for work as soon as we had finished eating. It was a snow day for us, so without school it meant a three day weekend! That made us really happy. We helped Mom clear the table and I asked, "Can I go out and play with Jimmy?"

Mom, replied "Yes." But I had to stay in hollering distance and needed to be back in time for lunch. And so I was off to Jimmy's house.

I had so much fun playing with Jimmy out in the snow. But my curiosity about how Dad would put a stop to the fox problem was on my mind the whole time. I was thinking about it all day. And just couldn't wait for him to get home.

Jimmy said, "I bet he's gonna put on a chicken costume and wait for them. And when the foxes try to eat him, he'll catch 'em and kill them doggone foxes!"

I said, "No, no, no. That's stupid!"

Jimmy looked a bit mad and said, "Alright Einstein, tell me what you think he will do?"

I said, "Maybe he will dig some pits around the chicken coop and put some crocodiles in them. And then when the foxes fall in, they will get eaten up!"

"That's stupid little Mac! Where is he gonna get crocodiles from!?"

I scrunched my face and shrugged my shoulders, "I don't know. Maybe at the crocodile store?" Jimmy looked real excited. I had really peaked his curiosity now!

Me and Jimmy had fun playing in the snow till lunch time. "I better get home for lunch before Mom tans my hide!" Jimmy knew just what that meant too. If there was anybody in Leeper Holler that had more tanning than me, it was Jimmy. Yeah, he was no stranger to a good switching!

So we made plans to go home for lunch and meet back up at the big hill later on. All I could think about was whether or not David would be at home when I got there. I said, "God, don't let David be home, don't let David be home!"

I said it twice, just in case God didn't hear me the first time. I repeated myself a lot, as many children do I suppose. But David, he was like a bad joke from the Devil. Or perhaps the Devil's way of ruining my childhood. Or he could have even been God's way of shaping me into the man that I am today. Who knows!

I walked into the house and saw that he wasn't sitting there at the table, as I had dreaded he would be. I took a gander around, no sign of him anywhere. "Thank you God!"

I better ask Mom to be sure. David was like a snake in the grass, he could be hiding anywhere. And suddenly, he would spring up and attack!

So I asked Mom if David was home and she told me, "No. He went to spend the night over at a cousin's house."

I started dancing around like an Indian on spirit water, shouting "Whoopi!! Hallelujah, praise God thank you Jesus!!"

You see, we were raised in a Pentecostal church, so when we thanked God, we thanked God! And we didn't hold nothing back. This was turning out to be a pretty good day. No school, no David, three day weekend, life couldn't be any better!

About that time my sister Kathy came in from the other room. She wasn't as bad as my brother David. He was like a wasp, if you got close to him he would sting you. But she was like a wolf, if you weren't in her territory bothering her, she would leave you alone.

She sat across the table from me. It was just me, her and Mom that day. I never did see much of my older brothers. Charles was always with his girlfriend and Kenny, who was a year younger had a car. So he was always out doing something. It seemed like the only time they came home was to sleep at night.

I remember thinking, 'I can't wait to be old enough to run off and never look back'. But now that I'm older and gone, it seems like all I ever do is look back! It was a simpler time. And though we were poor, we had a Mom and Dad that loved us. We fought a lot as brothers and sisters, but we didn't let anybody else mess with one another though.

I remember one time a bigger boy was picking on me in the holler. David came along and jumped in between us. He stood up for me and didn't let nobody pick on me. I hadn't seen that side of him before that day.

After lunch, I asked Mom, "Can I go back out and play with Jimmy?"

She said "Yes..."

"But stay in hollering distance." I finished her sentence.

She looked at me kinda sideways, with her eyes bugging out a bit. You know, that look that makes you rethink your motives. She said, "Make sure you come back before your Dad gets home from work."

And so me and Jimmy continued to play all day. After slipping and falling down in the snow, nearly breaking our necks a few times, we went back over to my house. Dad wasn't home yet, but we just couldn't wait until he was! So we went up to the chicken coop to wait for him. In the meantime, we decided to kick around some more ideas.

Jimmy said, "Maybe we could get some aliens to shoot them with their ray guns!"

"That's a good one!" I said. "How about we just try praying to God that he would keep the chickens safe?"

"I don't think your Dad is real big on religion."

"What do you mean by that Jimmy?" I asked him.

"Well, every time I have been over for dinner, it's always your Mom that says grace. And at the end, he never even said 'Amen' with everyone else."

Jimmy really got me to thinking about my Dad. I guess he was right. And it was always Mom kneeling down and praying, and telling us Bible stories for bedtime. I really didn't know how my Dad felt about God.

It was just then, that I heard Mr. Fisher's truck pull up. I could tell it was his because it had a funny knock in it. But he would help my Dad whenever he needed use of the truck. Dad taught me that a good friend is hard to find. But when you find one, they usually last a lifetime.

I gave Jimmy a nudge and he fell off the rock he was sitting on. I let out a giggle, but he didn't find it funny at all. We went down to see Dad pulling a big roll of something out of the back of Mr. Fisher's truck. I hadn't seen anything like it before. It looked like someone had picked a bunch of thorns and rolled them up in a big roll.

We got up close enough to see better and Dad told me, “Get back little Mac. That’s barb wire and it will stick you!”

Dad and Mr. Fisher ran a big stick through the roll and carried it up to the chicken coop. They covered the top of the coop with it. After they covered it all up, they stood back and looked it over. Dad had a real proud look on his face. It sure did look dangerous. Not only for us kids playing around the coop, but for the chickens too!

Though it sure looked dangerous to me, I was just a seven year old kid, so I shrugged it off. Mom stuck her head out of the back door and yelled, “Suppertime!”

Me and Jimmy told each other goodbye. Mr. Fisher looked at Dad and said, “I hope that works Otis?”

“I’m sure it will. No more feeding those foxes.” He said.

Mr. Fisher got in his truck and took off down the road. Dad threw his arm around my shoulder and said, “Come on little Mac, let’s go in and tie on the feed bag.”

That was a happy moment for me. I really liked it when my Dad would put his arm around me. He wasn’t a very emotional person. I don’t think I ever remember hearing him say, ‘I love you’. I do remember hearing him and Mom argue about that though. He would say to her, ‘I show them kids that I love them by putting a roof over their head, food on the table and shoes on their feet!'

Mom would reply and say to him, 'It wouldn't hurt nothing for you to tell them that you love them.' After growing up, I know what Mom said was true. Children are a gift from God. And we should treasure them every chance we get.

We walked into the back door of our shotgun house. The rest of the kids were already sitting at the table.

"Hurry and get washed up, everybody else is ready to eat!" We got ourselves seated. "Did you get that coop all fixed up?" Mom asked.

"Yeah. I guess so." Dad told her.

"You don't sound too sure about it?"

"I'm sure it's fixed." He said again.

But I wasn't too sure about it. I was worried about that barb wire hurting one of us kids. Or hurting the chickens. And especially our favorite rooster, Mr. Cock-a-doo! We sure did love him! My sister Kathy and I would go out and play with Mr. Cock-a-doo every night after supper. And after we ate and helped Mom clean up, Kathy asked me, "Do you wanna go play with Mr. Cock-a-doo little Mac?"

I said, "Sure do!"

So we went out the door and up to the chicken coop. Kathy went ahead and opened up the latch for us to get in. But she got her hand cut on that barb wire. And it was a bad cut. It looked pretty deep. She turned and asked me to latch the gate back. "I gotta go and get Mom to doctor up my hand little Mac!"

I could see that she was holding back the tears. She was pretty tough for an eight and a half year old girl. I would have been crying my eyes out! She had run ahead and I followed the blood trail all the way to the house. I went inside and said to Dad, "I thought that bob wire was dangerous!"

He said, "Your sister is gonna be just fine little Mac. And it's not bob wire, it's barb wire."

I followed Kathy and Mom back into the bedroom. Mom had opened up the bible to Ezekiel 16:6, and prayed the prayer for the blood to stop. And just as it had before, it worked! And the blood stopped. "Thanks to Jesus!" Mom said. I still can't believe how tough my sister was. She didn't even cry!

After we played some games as a family, we all got ready for bed around 8:30. Mom tucked us in and helped us say our prayers. I got up early the next morning to do my chores. It was Saturday, so it was my turn to feed the chickens. We had to get our chores done before we could eat. I liked to get my chores done before David got up. He liked to dump a bucket of water on my head, or push me down in the pig pen. So I would tip-e-toe past his bed not to wake him up. Then it was slowly through the door, closing it softly. Then to the root cellar to get some chicken feed.

I made my way up the hill to the coop with the feed and my eyes were not prepared for what I saw. Mr. Cock-a-doo was hanging from the top of the fence and his crop was caught in the barb wire! I was so upset, I didn't know what to do!

So I turned and ran back down to the house as fast as I could. I ran in the house and started shaking my Dad. "Wake up! Wake up! It's Mr. Cock-a-doo! Come fast!"

Kathy heard me and asked, "Is something wrong with Mr. Cock-a-doo?"

I said, "Yes, come quick!"

So the three of us went back up to the coop. Mr. Cock-a-doo was hanging there, motionless with blood on the snow beneath him.

Dad said to Kathy, "Go back to the house and get me a box. Put some newspaper in it and bring it to me!"

I said, "Dad, I told you that barb wire would get someone hurt!"

"Calm down little Mac." He told me.

But I couldn't calm down. I loved Mr. Cock-a-doo!

Kathy came back with the box and Dad pulled him out of the fence and put him in the box. He walked back down to the house and me and Kathy followed close behind. We were holding each other for comfort as we walked. Our eyes were pouring tears.

We walked in the house and Mom got out of bed. "How bad is it, Otis?" She asked.

"It's bad. He will never make it. His crop is torn off. *(The crop is how the chicken digests it's food.)*

Mom said "Never say never! We know a Doctor who can heal anything. His name is Jesus!"

Dad just shook his head as he walked away.

Mom called me and Kathy over to the bed. Kathy set the box with Mr. Cock-a-doo in it on the bed. Mom said, "My darlings, remember how we prayed for Kathy's hand last night? Now take off the wrapping and look at it."

Kathy took off the wrapping and the cut was gone.

Mom said, "Now God will do the same for Mr. Cock-a-doo!"

So me and Kathy laid our hands on him and began to cry out to God. After we had prayed to God and Mom had read that bible verse again, she told us to go wash up and eat something. But we weren't hungry. She told us to wash up anyways and go play so that God could do His work!

And so we played together all day. We didn't even argue one time that day. Before bedtime, we decided to go and pray one last time for Mr. Cock-a-doo. We laid our hands on him and this is what we prayed:

"Our Heavenly Father, we come to you in the name of Jesus. And by His stripes Mr. Cock-a-doo is healed!"

Then we went to bed, knowing in our hearts that he would be healed. The next morning about 6 o'clock, we heard the most joyful noise ever. It was like music to our ears. It was the sound of a rooster crowing in the house!

We heard Dad say, "What!! He's alive!?"

We cried out with joy, "Thank you Jesus!"

It was Mr. Cock-a-doo up on the edge of his box crowing. He lived for three good years after that. And Kathy and I knew that it was only by the grace of God that he had survived!

15

The Healing Spring

This is Little Mac, and it is the winter of 1965. It's about three degrees below zero outside, and there's about four inches of snow on the ground.

My friend, Jimmy, is staying the night with me. We are both twelve years old, and you know how two twelve year old boys are always looking for some kind of trouble to get into.

We've been outside most of the day running and playing in the snow. And that is just what we were doing when we heard Mama calling from the back porch for us to come in for supper. We both were mighty hungry so we took off running for the porch.

My sister, Kathy, met us at the back door, looking straight into Jimmy's eyes. "You can come into this house, but you are not gonna be taking your shoes off tonight!"

Now let me explain. My friend Jimmy is a real good kid, but his feet smell like a polecat. According to my sister they actually smell worse than that. One time when he stayed the night it took us almost two weeks to get the smell out of the house. It was like having a dead mouse in your house, but not being able to find it.

Jimmy stared at Kathy, he knew that she wasn't going to let him in the house unless he promised to leave his shoes on. He finally agreed, and Kathy let us in. But she still made him pinky promise.

We headed into the kitchen and poured some water into the wash basin to wash up for supper.

Jimmy leaned in close to me and whispered, "Little Mac, I can't sleep with my shoes on."

I whispered back to him, "We will just wait until she goes to bed, then you can take your shoes off." But I knew in my heart that the smell of his feet would wake her up, and probably everyone else in the house too! But I had to tell him something.

We sat at the table, said grace and started eating, but Kathy was giving Jimmy the evil-eye all through the meal. We were glad when we saw Grandpa through the window shoveling the walk to the chicken coop. Jimmy and I hurried up and ate our supper, then headed back outside.

I told Jimmy that if we helped Grandpa shovel snow that he might tell us a good story. My Grandpa was one of the best storytellers in the entire county. We asked him if he'd tell us a story if we helped him shovel snow, and he gladly agreed, and we went to work.

About thirty minutes later we were done, and about as cold as a couple of frogs in a November pond would have been.

"Let's go on in and get your Grandma to make some hot chocolate." Grandpa said as we followed him into his house. "Take a load off." He said as he pointed to the couch. Then he hollered at Grandma, "Come on woman! Make these boys some hot chocolate!"

"Crazy old man." We heard Grandma grumble under her breath, "I ought'ta hit you in the head with a skillet." We held back our giggles, knowing that Grandpa was hard of hearing.

We settled down and told Grandpa about Jimmy's problem with Kathy.

Grandpa chuckled, "She's probably got a crush on you."

Just then Grandma came back with the hot chocolate. "Don't you boys listen to that crazy old man, he don't know what he's talking about."

Grandpa reached over and smacked her right on her rump. "Why don't you go attend to woman's work. We got some men's business to attend to."

With that Grandma just turned and shook her head as she went back to the kitchen.

Jimmy and I were starting to giggle again when Grandpa turned back to us, "Now that we got that woman out of the way let's get on with that story.

"There used to be a man who lived here in the Holler that everyone called Jim Bob. Well he had an awful skin disease. All his skin was drawn and withered almost like he had been burned really bad over his whole body.

"He was always around, but one week in the year of 1940 he completely disappeared. People 'round here thought that maybe he had up and gone for good when he just as suddenly showed back up.

"Now everyone knew Jim Bob, but Jim Bob was different when he came back. All that burned up looking skin was completely healed and perfect. Old ugly Jim Bob was actually handsome, and that is exactly what the people of Leeper started to call him.

"Not long after he came back we got some time to sit down together, and I asked him, "How did this happen, Jim Bob?"

"Now these are the exact words that JimBob told me."

"Well I was out in the flat woods sipping on some of your moonshine. And I got really drunk, and fell into this spring running straight outta the hill. But I was so drunk that I couldn't pull myself out. So I just rested my head on the side and slept right there in the spring.

Well, when I woke the next morning I noticed that my skin was looking better. So I just stayed in there for the whole week. Every night my skin was healing and by the seventh day all that disease on my skin was gone.

That there water healed my skin! I swear on my mother's grave that is exactly what happened."

Grandpa looked at the both of us, "Now I've heard tales of lots of folks gettin' healed by that spring. Now you boys ought to be getting on home."

With that we headed out. About halfway home Jimmy stopped and looked at me, "Are you thinking what I'm thinking?"

I looked him square in the eyes, "I think we're both thinking exactly what Grandpa wanted us to be thinking." He had told that story to us for a reason. Grandpa knew that I knew where that healing spring was, because my cousin, Junior, and I had followed him to it before. We had found his moonshine still there at the healing spring the summer before.

We rushed over to my house, and there was Kathy, waiting at the front door, pointing her finger right at us. "I will throw you both out into the freezing cold, if I smell his feet even once tonight!" You could almost feel the anger coming from her.

Jimmy looked at me in a puzzled way, "I don't think she has a crush on me."

I had to hold my giggles back, “I don’t think so either buddy.”

As night fell and bedtime came, Mom said that we could sleep in the front room because she knew that my brother David didn’t get along with me or Jimmy. Se we made ourselves a cot on the floor with blankets. As everyone said their good-nights Jimmy and I knew what we had to do. Without so much as a word to each other, we knew that there was no other choice.

Slowly the house quieted as everyone fell asleep. Almost an hour after getting to bed, we were finally able to get up again. We got on our heavy coats and wrapped some heavy covers over top of that.

We knew that it was cold and dark out in the Flat woods, not just scary and completely evil.

We grabbed a couple of flashlights off the ice box as we crept out the back door.

Once outside I broke the silence and blurted out our first word in over an hour. “Jimmy!”

“What Little Mac?” Jimmy’s voice was shaky.

“What if we freeze to death, or what if there is something evil in them Flat woods and it carries us off, or kills us?”

A sad look crossed Jimmy’s face as he turned away from me, “Either way, no one will call me ‘stinky feet’ any more.”

And with that we started for the Flat woods, not knowing what it would have in store for us that cold, cold night. Jimmy and I had heard the warnings, ‘Never, ever go into the Flat woods at night’. Yet here we were headed straight for the center of them at eleven-thirty. By the time we would get there it would be full on midnight, what Grandpa called ‘the witching hour’.

Up the first hill we went, then down into the valley, up the next hill. Every step taking us closer to our doom, or to the healing that Jimmy needed. That was what kept us going, though we were constantly turning and looking behind us, expecting to see something there creeping behind the trees.

At some point Jimmy’s teeth started chattering so hard that I could hear them. I didn’t know if it was from the cold or if he was just that scared. I kept asking him to turn back, but he had set his determination on that healing spring.

Now any good country boy knows, that if he is going out into the woods, to carry matches with him. Well Jimmy must not have been too good of a country boy, because he forgot his. But, luckily for us, I didn’t. We pulled down some dead twigs off a nearby tree, cleared an area on the ground and started as small fire to warm up our hands.

In the distance a wolf began to howl. The hairs on the back of our necks stood up. We just knew that it was the wolves that had been creeping behind us. Several more joined in the howling. We built the fire up a little bigger, we had been told that the fire would keep the wolves away. And everyone had heard the story of the boy on all fours, so now we were too scared to leave our fire.

But we were not going to give up. Pretty soon we warmed up. Jimmy stood and looked at me, "No time like the present." He turned and walked over to the spring and cracked some ice off the top. Being a running spring only the surface would freeze.

Jimmy looked worried as he sat down on a rock by the water's edge and pulled off his shoes and socks. Slowly he put his feet toward the water and let one big toe touch the top. He jerked back and looked at me, "Little Mac, that water is cold!"

"Oh, stop being a girl and just do it. Like when you go swimming and jump right into the cold water. Do it quick." But I was secretly thanking God that it wasn't me sticking my feet into that ice cold water.

Jimmy took a deep breath and plunged his feet right into the water. "Hey, it's not as cold as I thought. Come on over here Little Mac, we'll have a foot-washing party."

"No thank you. I am going to stay right here sitting by the fire and keeping an eye out for them wolves." I said sternly.

We made up our minds that it was going to be an all nighter. The north wind kept blowing, and the wolves kept on howling. Somewhere around two it began to snow lightly. "Please God give me a break." I said quietly. All the while thinking that we didn't have a chance. That we are either going to freeze to death of be eaten alive by the wolves. One way or the other I knew that we were done for.

The hours crept on. The wolves howling, wind blowing and snow swirling. I fought to keep the fire going.

Sometime in the early morning hours I fell asleep, wrapped in the cover that I had brought from home. I don't know how long I had been out for but I sat straight up and looked around. God had kept His mighty hand upon us and kept us safe!

Jimmy was sound asleep on his rock with his feet dangling into the spring. I hurried over to him, "Jimmy, Jimmy wake up. We gotta get home! Mom gets up at six, and if we ain't there when she gets up..."

He looked at me wide-eyed, then jumped up, dried his feet and rushed to get his socks and shoes back on.

We ran for home as the sky began to slowly get lighter. Jimmy kept saying how his feet were hurting, but he toughed it out and didn't slow down any. Relief washed over us as we stood at my back door panting to catch our breath and the house was quiet.

Slowly we opened the back door, put our flashlights on top of the ice box and tip-e-toed back to our cots on the living room floor.

Almost the moment we got settled in, we heard Mom get up. "That was a close one." Jimmy whispered. I nodded quickly and pulled the covers tight.

A miracle happened that night, two young boys found the closest friendship that any boys could ever have. That friendship lasted until Jimmy turned fourteen, that's when Jimmy and his parents moved to New York City. And I never heard from or saw Jimmy ever again. But up until that day his feet never stunk again, and my sister, Kathy, would even let him take his shoes off in the house!

Thank you Jimmy for letting me know what true friendship really is.

16

The Indian Graveyard

It is a quiet May afternoon in the sleepy little town of Leeper. The flowers are blooming and the birds are singing, you can almost feel love in the air. Well, for everyone but me. I am Little Mac and I don't care one hoot for all that 'yucky stuff'. It's the early sixties, I'm only ten and all I care about is finding me an adventure!

Right about now I am sitting here in front of Judge Lucy's General Store waiting for my cousin Junior. His parents are going to drop him off in Leeper so that he can spend the night with me. Now Junior is more than just my cousin, he is one of my best friends and my partner in adventure!

As I waited, I decided to go and see what the four old men sitting on the far end of the porch were doing. They were all gathered around a checkerboard, sitting on top of old pickle barrels. The way they were hollerin' and stomping their feet youd'a thought that it was the world series of checkers going on.

All of the sudden the screen door of the General Store flew open! The old men suddenly quieted down, and looked respectfully toward the door. It was Old Judge Lucy himself standing in the doorway.

Now, I don't know if he was a real judge or not, but everyone around treated Judge Lucy with respect. I had even heard a story about how years ago a couple of men thought that they would go and rob Judge Lucy's store. But on that day he was judge, jury and the executioner all-in-one. When he got done with them, all those guys needed was a couple of six-foot deep holes.

"Quiet down out here! You are scaring all my customers away." He shouted from where he stood in the doorway. They all started laughing, even Judge Lucy. I didn't get whatever it was that they were laughing about, but I guess they did.

What I did understand was that this was my chance to make a nickel. Those old men thought that it was good luck to rub a cotton-top's head, at least that is what old Mr. Benjamin had told me. Sometimes they would ask me to sing a song for them and pay me a nickel for it. So I put on my sweetest face and walked over to them.

"Well, if it ain't Little Mac." Mr. Shelton said, "I got a quarter here for ya, cotton-top, if you sing 'I've Got A Mansion Over The Hilltop'" Well, that just happened to be one of my favorite songs, and a quarter back then would buy a lot of candy.

As I sang my heart out, the whole town seemed to stand still and listen to me. Mr. Shelton cheerfully gave me the quarter, rubbed my head for luck and sent me on my way. Straight into the store I went and got me a candy bar, an ice cream, a bag of potato chips and a soda, and I still had a nickel to spare.

I came out of the store just in time to see my cousin Junior getting there. He looked at me with big sad eyes. "Where's mine?" So I gave him the nickel that I had left over so he could get an ice cream for himself, and we would split the rest.

Just as Junior was coming out of the store with his ice cream we heard a ruckus from up the road. We soon realized that it was someone talkin' loudly, and fast, to themselves. I was pretty sure I knew who it was, since only one person around talked that fast.

"Come on, Junior." I said as I quickly jumped from the porch and headed for some bushes that were a little further up the road. We ducked behind the bushes and looked to see who it was.

I was right, it was an old one-armed man called Tuffy. Now I don't think anyone knew how old Tuffy was, he could have been a hundred for all I knew. But that didn't matter to me, I loved talking to him. He had some of the greatest stories I had ever heard. But most people around won't even talk to him because ever since he lost his arm in a sawmill accident he's been the town wino.

I know that he drinks too much and that some of his stories are probably completely made up, but he is my friend and I am proud to call him that. Just not in front of my Mom, or she would bust my butt!

We ran back to the General Store porch and sat down to wait. We knew that somehow or another we would have to get a story out of Tuffy. He was just now passing the bushes that we had been hiding in a minute before. He was walking fast like always, a few seconds later he was on the porch.

“Hi Little Mac. Hi Junior.” He said as he walked past. He didn’t bother saying anything to the old men playing checkers. He knew that there was no sense in doing so, they would just have something hurtful to say to him. I’d heard the things that they had said before. Things like, ‘Take a bath you dirty bum! You smell like a polecat! ain’t you got no water at your house?’.

It made me sad how mean they were to him, but old Tuffy paid them no mind. He just walked on past and into the store, going after his morning wine.

We sat for about thirty minutes waiting for him to come back out, we figured he was in there talking to Judge Lucy. The Judge was one of the only people around who was nice to him, but I guess he had to be since he was a customer.

We just sat there waiting, but he still didn’t come out. Finally we decided to head in looking for him. One of the old men playing checkers hollered at us. “Hey, if you’re looking for that crazy old Tuffy, he probably snuck out the back door. He likes to head across the tracks and drink out behind the feed store.”

"You boys really need to stay away from that old wino. He is going to get you both into trouble." Mr. Shelton told us.

I looked at him and nodded. "Yes sir," I said with a smile, "We get ourselves into the trouble, Tuffy just tells us where we can find it." With that, Junior and I started giggling as we walked away.

We headed straight across the tracks and behind the feed store, but old Tuffy wasn't there. We saw Tom working on the feed dock. "Have you seen Tuffy?"

"Yeah, he headed over toward the mill pond." Tom said.

Now we just couldn't wait to hear a good story, so we ran the rest of the way there. When we got to the mill pond, there was Tuffy sitting on the ground under a big oak tree. He smiled real big at us.

"Come on boys, sit your butts down."

We sat down right beside him as he took a swig of his wine. "Let me guess, you boys wanna hear a story?" We nodded happily.

"Well, about a week ago me and Doc was sitting around at his house. It was really late at night and we was getting pretty loopy. (That means drunk, in Tuffy's speech.) When Doc said,

"You know I used to do a lot of 'coon hunting, but I ain't been in a while, you wanna go?"

Well that sure sounded like a good time to me so I told him, "Sure, but I ain't got me no gun."

"Well, I got two."

Doc said as he grabbed one rifle and handed me another.

We headed out the house and up the hill with our rifles, and we certainly didn't forget our drinks. Doc had his moonshine and I had my wine."

"Wait a minute!" Junior interrupted him. "How did you carry a rifle and your bottle of wine?"

"Well," Tuffy said. "I held the wine in my good hand and put the rifle under my stump. I'd rather drop the gun and shoot Doc or my foot than drop my wine and break it. Now why don't you jus' let me tell my story." We both shut our mouths and nodded 'yes'.

"So, we was headed up the big hill. I fell down a couple of times, but somehow managed not to shoot anyone. Now I'd say it was round about midnight when we reached the old water tower.

"Now I know you have heard the stories about the old water tower being built on that Indian graveyard and how the water there was no good. It always smelled and tasted like something died in it. We were all glad when the Leeper Mayor had it drained back in '43.

"But the tale goes, that at midnight, all them Indians come out of their graves and do a war dance. And there better not be any white folk around ‘cause the Indians will kill ‘em.

“We had just reached the tower when we started hearing something behind us. We turned around slowly and standing there in full war paint was an Indian Chief, wearing buffalo hide pants and a headdress full of feathers! He was just standing there looking like a beautiful, but deadly painting. He had his bow at full draw and pointed right at us. I thought that I was going to die!

“Just then Doc raised his rifle and let loose on the Chief. It knocked Doc right back onto his butt! But it only made the Indian Chief mad. We then did something I didn’t think we’d ever do. We dropped our guns and our drinks, and ran for the big oak next to the water tower.

“Now I had a little trouble climbing, as I only have the one good arm, but somehow I managed to dig in with that stump of mine and make it to where the tree leaned over the old water tower.

“Just as we reached the top, that Indian started running round and round letting out some sort of war cry. ‘Go into the tower!’ I hollered at Doc. He just looked at me. ‘He’ll just pick us off with that bow.’ Then Doc got up and started to climb down in the tower.

“We could see some old steel rods sticking out of the sides that we were able to use as foot holds and shimmy our way to the bottom. So there we sat in the dark, at the bottom of an old drained out water tower with nothing to drink listening to a crazed Indian war chief whooping and hollering.

"At some point we managed to fall asleep. The daylight woke us. It was quiet all around as we made our way back to the top of the tower. There was no Indian in sight as we climbed back down the tree.

First thing once we were down was to get a big drink and then pick up our rifles. We hurried back to Doc's house. On the way we made up our minds to never go back to the old water tower after midnight again."

Junior and I were quite excited as we jumped up from the ground and told Tuffy goodbye. Now if you remember what I told Mr. Shelton, Tuffy didn't get us into any trouble at all. He only told us where to go to get ourselves into trouble.

17

The Warts Boy

It was a cold morning on October 31st, 1963. The fire in the old King heater was roaring! Little Mac was running around the house, overcome with excitement. It was Halloween after all. And he was just sure that he was gonna win that costume contest! Yep. There wasn't no doubt about it.

Even though he was nine years old, this was the first real costume that little Mac ever had. His Mom had stayed up all night working on it. Now up until this point, all he had before was a paper bag over his head, with little eye holes cut out.

But not this year! Little Mac was going to be a clown! And he just loved his clown costume! Little Mac's Mom called him from the kitchen, "Little Mac, come eat your food before it gets cold!"

When he got to the dining room, he saw that his brother David was already sitting. Now David thought that his job in life was to make little Mac's life miserable. And let me tell you, he took his job serious.

After taking his seat, little Mac began to express his excitement about the contest. "I'm gonna win I tell ya, I just know I'm gonna win that contest!"

David laughed and looked over at little Mac, "You little moron! To win first place in the contest, you gotta be in a costume so good, that no one can even tell who you are!" Little Mac slowly sank in his seat.

"You can put some paint on your ugly face to make it look like a clown. You can put that clown costume on your ugly little body. But if you don't do something about them wart covered hands, everyone will know who you are!"

The look of excitement had completely left little Mac's face. And it was replaced with the look of despair. You see, little Mac had a lot of warts on his hands. And the kids in town had even made up a song about it. The tune was something like…

'Here comes little Mac, walking down the road. He ended up at the creek, playing with the toads. Little Mac should have done what little Mac was told! The frog went pee pee on his hands, here comes the warts boy, the warts boy, the warts boy!'

And then they would all have a laugh. Oh, the horrible sound of that laughter ringing in his head! Little Mac jumped up from the table and ran to his room. He threw himself across his bed and began to cry.

After getting on to David, Mom went and got a pair of Dad's old work gloves and came in to little Mac's room. Mom always had just the right words to say. "Listen here little Mac, God makes everyone a little different. So don't you worry about being perfect, no one is. You wear your costume proudly because I sewed love into every stitch. And you take these gloves and wear them over your hands."

Little Mac jumped up out of bed with the return of excitement! Mom had done it again. She wrapped and healed the wounds of childhood. Little Mac gave his Mom a kiss on the cheek to say, 'Thanks for always being there!' He took his gloves, his costume and his lunch and headed out the door for school.

He didn't get very far down the road though, when suddenly he heard the sound of laughter behind him. He looked back. Oh no, It was David and his friend Little Boy! They ran up and snatched his gloves from his pocket.

"Oh no, God no!" Little Mac began to pray.

Mom worked so hard on that costume, but now he had no way to cover up my imperfect hands! All little Mac could do, was think of the song his Mom was singing as she was making the costume, 'Amazing Grace.' He just kept on walking down the road.

When he got to school, he could hear all the kids asking the teacher, "When can we put on our costumes?" But little Mac was in no hurry at all. He just kept thinking about what his Brother David had told him.

Time seemed to be dragging. The minutes were like hours. He couldn't stop thinking about what would happen when the time came to put on his costume. Finally, the teacher announced, "It's time for the costume contest!"

Little Mac's heart began to throb with fear. The teacher asked the students, "How many of you do not have a costume today?"

There were three kids that raised their hands. Two of them were his enemies, Ricky and Cecil. The other one was little Susie, she was a girl Little Mac had a crush on. The teacher said, "No one will be left out of the contest, so you three can be our Judges!"

'Oh no!' Thought little Mac.

Miss Reed said, "Boys can change in the art room, girls can go and change in the spare classroom."

Everyone grabbed their costumes and began to walk to their assigned rooms. Little Mac felt like he was about to throw up. He was terribly nervous. As he walked by the Judges, little Susie flashed him a smile. That calmed his nerves. Only Susie or Mom could have had such an effect.

After everyone got their costumes on, they came together and lined up in front of the classroom. Little Mac was getting nervous again. He began to think, 'They will know who I am. They will see the warts on my hands and know it's me.'

He was all the way down at the end of the line. And the Judges started on the opposite end. They were knocking them down like flies! It was like they had x ray vision, because they were calling out names left and right.

There were only two students left now. Little Susie flashed Little Mac another smile. He thought she knew who he was. She turned to the other Judges and said, "It's gotta be little Mac or Billy, I just can't tell!"

Little Mac was sweating like a pig.

"Get outta the way! I can tell you who it is!" Said Cecil. He looked him up and down. And up and down again. And at that moment, a big evil grin came across his face.

He walked over and whispered something into Ricky's ear. Little Mac knew this was bad news for him. And he was right. Because just then, they began to sing that HORRIBLE song:

'Here comes little Mac, walking down the road. He ended up at the creek, playing with the toads. Little Mac should have done what little Mac was told! The frog went pee pee on his hands, here comes the warts boy, the warts boy, the warts boy!'

Little Mac just couldn't hold the tears back. He started to cry as the laughter filled the room. He couldn't think of anything to do. So he ran out of the room to escape the laughter. Down the long hallway he went. And two miles up the road to his front door. He was so tired by the time he got there, it was all he could do to open it.

He had run home to Mom, the only one who could understand. But hopefully, she wouldn't be upset about him leaving school early. This would be a worse end to an already bad day if she gave him a whooping!

After he told her the story, she took him by the hand and led him out the front door. He thought, 'Now I'm really gonna get it!' She said, "You see your Grandpa out there in the yard little Mac, go down and tell him your story."

So little Mac walked down to where his Grandpa was sitting in the yard. Grandpa had a lot of things happen for him that couldn't be explained. Like a medicine man, or someone with healing power.

As he walked up Grandpa said, "Cami, why aren't you in school?"

Now Cami was an old lady that lived in Leeper Holler. She was about 1,000 years old. Grandpa liked to call her my girlfriend, because he knew it made me angry.

"I am not Cami and she is not my girlfriend!"

He let out a little giggle, like that had just made his day. He looked me right in the eyes and said, "What can I do for you today little Mac?"

So Little Mac told Grandpa his story. And Grandpa had pity on him. "Let me see your hands there little Mac."

Grandpa took both of little Mac's hands into one of his big hands.

"Let me count them there warts on your hands."

And so he counted, one all the way to thirty two!

"I tell you what I want you to do little Mac. Go home and do not eat. Go straight to bed and do not get up until tomorrow morning. All them warts will be gone."

Little Mac said, "Grandpa, it's only 2:30!"

He said, "Don't argue with me. If you want them warts to be gone, do as I have said."

So without saying another word, little Mac went home and straight to bed. Grandpa must have come and talked to Mom, because she never even called for supper time. He felt like Grandpa had a spell put on him, because he slept the whole night through. And it was the best sleep he had ever had. And when Little Mac woke up, to his surprise, all of them warts were gone! No more songs, no more laughter, no more warts!

He asked Grandpa what he had done. Grandpa told him, "I am the seventh son of a seventh son, which gives me power." He never figured out what exactly that meant, but he sure was thankful for what he did.

In loving memory of my Grandpa Charlie Laxton. Thank you for being a special person!

18

Grandpa's Headless Man

It's a hot August day in a sleepy little town called Leeper. It's 1961 and my name is Little Mac. The day is hot as ever, and dragging by. I was bored so I went in the kitchen to talk to my Mom.

"Hey Mom, I'm so sweaty and bored!"

"Get out from under my feet little Mac, I'm bunin' up too! Why don't you go out in the backyard and talk to your Grandpa."

It was so hot in our house because we didn't have any air conditioning. We had an old tin roof, it was a slab lumber house and it only had one fan in it! So when it was 100 degrees outside, it felt like 120 degrees on the inside!

So of course I was happy to go and see Grandpa! And I ran out the house as fast as my little legs could carry me!

Now Grandpa only lived right down the gravel road from us. You could throw a rock and hit his house from ours. In fact, I tried it once. The rock went right through the front window! Of course, Grandma was not too happy about it. But Grandpa told her "Shut up old lady! Boys will be boys." And that was the end of that.

He told Grandma to go and get me a cup of tea so we could sit and drink together under the shade tree. He sure did like his red root tea. And the best thing about it, was that it was free! Right out there in them woods. All you had to do was get out there and pick it.

Grandpa and Grandma sure did a lot of hollering back and forth at one another. I guess after 40 years of marriage and 15 kids, they were used to it. Grandma gave me a cup and asked with love in her eyes, "How you doing little Mac?"

I nodded as to say, "I'm okay."

Then I went out to where Grandpa was under the tree. He said, "Have a seat here beside me."

So I sat down right next to him. He put his arm around me and coughed a few times. He said, "You know I started smoking when I was about ten years old. I always knew it was gonna kill me one day, but it was a habit I just couldn't quit. *(Grandpa died a few years later of lung cancer.)*

"Well, I guess we can sit here in the shade, drink some tea and I'll tell you a story."

I just loved it when Grandpa would tell his stories, even though they did seem to scare me a bit!

"Have you ever heard the legend of the headless man, little Mac?"

I shook my head and said, "No."

"Back in 1925 there was a man by the name of Billy D. that lived here in Leeper. But he worked just over in Mill Spring. He didn't have a car, like most people and he walked a stretch of railroad tracks back and forth to work everyday. Now this Billy, he had a bit of a drinking problem. He would drink every day after work in a little bar there in Mill Spring.

"Well, one day he got himself a little more drunk than usual and stumbled out of the bar about dusk.

"The woman that was running the bar ran out after him. 'Hey, why don't you have someone take you home?'

"'No, I need to walk to sober up. The little lady don't like it when I drink so much.'

"And so he staggered off toward the railroad tracks and disappeared into the night. Now after working all day in the heat, that alcohol took a real toll on him. And he was mighty tired. He sat down on the long straight stretch of the tracks just to rest a bit.

“He stretched out and rested his head on the track and was out like a rock! He never even heard that train coming!

“Now when he never made it home, his wife got some of the town folk to go out looking for him. So they set out on the tracks that he always walked home after work. Sure enough, they found his head in no time. And his body was just a ways down the tracks.

“Now most folks are scared of that stretch of the tracks. They say every night around about seven o’clock in the evening time, Old Billy will be out there walking that stretch of the railroad tracks. Myself, I hadn’t never seen no ghost and pretty sure I wouldn’t be scared even if I did.

“Well, one day I was working for farmer Brown out on his farm in Mill Spring. We had been planting some corn in his field. He started complaining that rain was going to be moving in over night and he didn’t have enough seed to finish the field up.

“‘If it rains we can’t get the seed in for days, it will be too doggone wet! And I can’t get the seed because my doggone truck is broke down!’ I said, ‘Don’t worry there Mr. Brown, I’ll go into Leeper and get the seed.’

“‘Charlie, I know that you are a big man, but how will you carry two 50 pound bags all the way from Leeper?’

“‘Don’t you worry, I will pack them back on my shoulders.’ And so I took off to get the seed. After I left the feed store, it was about 6:45. And by the time I got on that straight stretch of the tracks, all I could think about was what all those people had said about the ghost of old Billy walking the tracks at night. And it was about 7 o'clock now!

"Even though I never did believe it, all of a sudden, there it was. Right in front of me!! The ghost of Billy walking with his head in his hands! I decided to set the seed bags down next to the tracks and sit on them till he passed by.

"You just sat there!? You didn't run!?" I asked Grandpa.

"No little Mac. I just sat there and when he got close enough to pass by, I spoke to him!"

"'Good evening. Looks like we might have some rain moving in!' I said to Billy.

"To my surprise, Billy turned his head and said, 'Gotta get home to the little lady. She don't like it when I drink. I got to take a nap before I get home.'

"With a puzzled look on my face I said, 'Okay.' And he just kept on walking down the tracks. I picked up the bags of seed, threw them on my shoulders and went back to farmer Brown's. That was the first and last time that I ever seen a ghost."

And that was the last time Grandpa ever told me a story. He lost a three year battle with cancer. It's sad what those cigarettes will do to a man. He was 6'3" 225 pounds. The cancer took him down to only 125 pounds before he died. Those cigarettes deprived me of many good years I could have spent with my Grandpa.

19

The Box Hole Screamer

Around the sleepy town of Leeper, Missouri there are many old tales and legends. Some are scary, some interesting, and some are completely unbelievable!

Now this is the story of what happened to a couple of my good friends in the holler way back in the mid-sixties. To understand what happened to these men, we have to go back and learn the legend.

Right outside of Leeper runs the mighty Black River. There is a place where the river splits and a mile downriver meets back up with itself, making an island. At it's widest the island is about a half a mile wide. Its overgrown with brush and very wild. But with an island that large, at the down-river side is a pretty slow turning current that the fish just love! This place is called "the box hole."

It was a hot July day back in 1935, when a group of ten teenagers from Piedmont decided to come downriver to fish and camp out on the box hole island. A young man by the name of Einar (which ironically means 'lone warrior') was the only one left to tell the tale.

He told an incredible story. "We set our boats in the water in the late afternoon. After almost an hour we came to the only fork in the river and veered to the right to make landfall on the island.

"We tied up the boats and began to make our way south to the box hole. A couple of the boys, including myself, had brought along our machetes. But it was still slow work making our way down to the box hole. By the time we got there the evening shadows had set in.

"Us boys with the machetes went to work making sure the area was good and clear to set up the tents and make a campfire. By the time tents were set up and a fire was going, it was good and dark. But the moon was big and full and gave lots of light, so we went ahead and started fishing.

"Now we had heard the stories of the 'Screamer', about how it was half-wolf half-man, even how it never left anything alive that came on it's island. But we didn't believe such a silly story.

"We had heard stories about the great fishing down at the box hole. Those we had believed, some of us had even been down here with our dads in the daytime to fish. It was just a weedy overgrown island.

"So we were having a good time catching some big fish, cooking them up and eating them right there at our fire. It was getting pretty late and we were talking about going to our tents when John looked at his watch and loudly said, 'Well, it is just about midnight. I guess in fifteen minutes we are gonna see if the Screamer is really real.'

"We had been having a good time, but the tales of the Screamer was in the back of all of our minds. Now we had to face our fear. We all got real quiet and looked around, even with the big moon it was still very dark and shadowy. One of the boys across from me laughed nervously. 'John, you know that story is a bunch of..'

"A loud splashing noise cut him off, it sounded like something huge swimming toward the island. Suddenly the splashing stopped and something let out a horrid scream, like a woman in great pain. I grabbed my machete and held it tight.

"John started putting more wood on the fire. They say 'It won't come near the fire.' I could hear the fear in his voice.

"We heard heavy steps running toward the camp, the thing charged through the camp and leaped straight into the fire, rose up on it's hind legs and roared.

"It's teeth were long and sharp, it's claws massive. It glared at us as it stood in the fire, it looked almost as if the fire was making it bigger and stronger. It let out one more horrible screaming roar and my friends began to scream and scatter. I was stunned, I didn't know what to do. I dropped to my knees and began to pray to God to help us.

"The beast sprang from the fire and came right for me. It stopped just short and leaned down and began to smell me, I could feel it's hot breath on my face. Suddenly it raised up and took off running in another direction.

"I jumped up and ran for my tent grabbing my machete and flashlight on the way. I got my backpack from the tent and took off toward the boats. When I got there something had gashed massive holes into them, they were not usable at all.

"I turned and ran for the south end of the island. I knew that the town of Mill Spring wasn't too far away. I could hear my friends screaming but I ran and leaped into the water. I swam as fast as I could and then I floated for a little ways.

"Soon I was at the Mill Spring bridge. I made my way to the shore and ran the half mile to town. I don't know how my legs made it there, but they did.

"The next day the authorities went out to search the island. They found absolutely nothing. No boats, no bodies, no teenagers or fishing gear and no screamer."

So we come back to my story. I'm Little Mac, I was born in the Holler in 1953 and raised in the Holler until I left in 1974 at the age of twenty-one. Now I had some good friends in Leeper, but not a one was a better storyteller then Tuffy, an old one-armed wino who lived at the end of the road through town. People around town didn't like Tuffy much at all. They would even cross the street just so that they wouldn't have to walk near him. But I counted him as one of my good friends.

On that day the events were seen by many. Tuffy woke that morning wanting some fish. His neighbors had seen him digging worms out by his chicken coop. Soon after he headed down the road to Doc Hurley's house. Before long the old men were seen carrying some fishing gear on their way to Judge Lucy's General Store.

Judge Lucy said that Tuffy and Doc stopped in to buy a bottle of wine and to see if they could borrow his little aluminum row boat. He said that they were arguing about the Screamer, that Doc was worried but Tuffy just kept telling him that it was a bunch of baloney. The Judge joked with them for a few minutes and told them not to get his boat all clawed up. Which only made old Doc Hurley fret even worse as they headed out the back to get Judge Lucy's boat.

Townspeople said that they had seen the old men with the boat slung between the two of them by a rope, their fishing gear, wine and moonshine in the boat. They were walking through town arguing as they headed for the Black River. Doc worrying as Tuffy shook his stump and hollered. They said that you could even hear Tuffy shouting as the little boat splashed into the water and the oar-beats began.

The next day around noon-time Judge Lucy began to wonder why them old drunks hadn't come back with his boat. He closed up shop and headed up the road. No one answered at Doc's place. Further up the road at Tuffy's was no answer either.

Judge Lucy grabbed a couple of men from town and headed out. They searched the river as they followed it south all they way to the box hole island where they finally spotted the borrowed boat, but the men were nowhere in sight.

They searched the island and found Tuffy in the thickest undergrowth in the very center of the island. He was covered from head to toe with deep cuts and scratches. But Doc was not anywhere on the island.

From the look of things at the box hole the two men had been doing some good fishing when they decided to shore the boat and drink for a while. Marks in the dirt under a large old oak looked as if the two men had laid down to rest for a bit, and whatever happened to them was after that.

They took Tuffy back to Leeper and there got word that Doc Hurley had been found down at the Mill Spring bridge perfectly unharmed, but scared out of his mind. Both were taken to the hospital, Doc was released a short time later but Tuffy had over a hundred stitches and had to be given blood.

When he was released things were never the same. The two men who had been best friends never spoke to each other again.

Tuffy became so bad with his drinking that he tried to drink rubbing alcohol and ended up being sent to a psychiatric ward in Farmington, Mo. Where he passed away some time later.

Doc Hurley's mind began to slip and his family came and took him home to Des Arc, Mo. He passed away there a few months later from advanced cancer.

I sure miss those crazy old men.

In loving memory of Doc and Tuffy. May you both rest in peace. Thanks for the memories!

20

The Attic

There was one thing that always scared me as a kid. I lost many hours of sleep just staring at it. My name is little Mac. And I am talking about the attic above my parents bed. I slept next to my sister Kathy across the room. Late at night, I would sometimes wake up from having bad dreams. They were horrible nightmares! I don't like to think about them very often, but I am going to tell you about one that has never left my mind.

It was a rainy night. And the lightning lit up the sky. The sound of the thunder was so loud that it shook the old tin roof. It sounded like someone was walking around up in the attic. Just back and forth, over and over again.

I was looking at the attic door and could almost clearly see long skinny fingers with claws sticking through the door and the wood. It could unhook the lock if it really wanted to. I prayed, 'God, don't let that thing come down here and eat me!'

The door opened, I saw it's glowing red eyes looking down. It was swinging it's claws at my Mom and Dad. I felt the puke come up in my throat! I just knew that as soon as it got done over there, it was going to come after me and Kathy!

I wanted to wake Kathy up, but I couldn't move. I was frozen in fear. It turned around and looked at me, with blood all over it's fur. It leaped off the bed and started toward me. There was a loud thump, every time it took a step. My heart was beating a hundred miles an hour.

It came and stood over my bed, looking down at me. It raised it's monstrous claws back and started to swing down on me.

At that moment, I heard Kathy's voice, "Wake up! You're screaming in your sleep little Mac!"

I couldn't get back to sleep all night. I just lay there staring at that attic door. As young as I was, I had made up my mind about it. I was going to go up there in that attic and see what was there. I had to put a stop to all these bad dreams and sleepless nights!

The next morning I had breakfast after doing my chores. After that, I was off to Jimmy's house. I told him the whole story, bad dreams and all. After telling him that I was going to go up there and look around the attic.

He said, “Count me in! I’m down!”

I was glad to have a partner that would go with me!

Jimmy said, “We have to come up with a plan first. When will your Mom and Dad be gone? How are we going to protect ourselves while we’re up there?”

“This is Friday, Mom and Dad go shopping today.” I told him.

“Yeah but don’t they make you go shopping with them?” Asked Jimmy.

“Sometimes they do.” I replied. Then scratched my head and thought for a moment.

“You think your Mom would write a note saying that I am staying with you at your house while they go shopping Jimmy?”

“Heck, why even bother getting my Mom to write a note, I can write the note for her!” My eyes got really wide when he said that.

“Isn’t that lying Jimmy?”

“Lies come out of your mouth. This is on a note, so it’s not the same as lying.”

I thought that made sense.

"So it's not us saying it, it's the note. Okay, that sounds cool to me!"

So Jimmy went and got a pad and pencil and wrote the note for me. He signed it in his Mom's name.

"Now, we need to get some protection for ourselves little Mac."

"I know what we can do. My brother Charles keeps a machete underneath his car seat. And my Mom keeps two flashlights on the bedside table!"

"I got one better than that." Said Jimmy.

"My Dad keeps his service revolver in his bedside table drawer."

With a terrified look on my face I asked:

"A gun! Isn't that a little dangerous for two eight year old boys!"

Jimmy, with a proud look on his face, said:

"Yes, a gun! My Dad taught me all about guns and how to use them."

"Okay." I replied. But I still wasn't sure that having a gun was a good idea.

We walked back down the holler to my house and gave Mom the note. With a gentle smile on her face, she looked at Jimmy and said:

"It's okay, as long as your Dad isn't at home." You see, Jimmy's Dad was a drunkard. And when he was drunk, he would sometimes beat Jimmy. And for that reason, my Mom did not like him. And she sure didn't want me to be around him.

After that, we simply turned around and walked out the door. I didn't say a word. I knew that if I did, Mom would have seen right through me. And I would have spilled the beans.

I was fairly quiet on the walk back to Jimmy's house. I guess I had a feeling of guilt come upon me. It felt like the sun going down, with that heavy darkness weighing down the light. Though I was young, I had learned that one little lie can quickly add up into many lies. And I could hear my Dad saying, 'A man is no better than his word'.

"Why you so quiet little Mac?" Jimmy asked me.

"Well Jimmy, I guess I feel bad about lying to my Mom."

"I told you little Mac, It wasn't us doing the lying, it was the note!"

"I think it's the same as lying though Jimmy."

We walked into Jimmy's house and went straight to his Dad's room. We got the service revolver from out of the drawer. I knew it was another mistake. And they really seemed to be adding up!

We went back to my house and stood behind the bushes, waiting for my Mom and Dad to go shopping. My brother Charles came out and was piddling in his car for a bit.

I told Jimmy, "We need to get that machete out of his car before he takes off." He walked back into the house.

"Let's get it!" I said.

I ran over to the car as fast as I could. Jimmy just stayed back in the bushes, like a scared little rabbit. I got the machete and was back in a flash! It was a good thing too. Because Charles was only in the house for a moment. He came back out and left quickly. So we waited for about a half an hour before Mom and Dad came outside to leave. One by one they came out of the house. But I hadn't seen my brother Kenny come out. If he was staying at home, that would really ruin our plans!

The car started up. I was beginning to get really nervous and worried. Just then, Kenny came running out and jumped in the car. They all took off out of the driveway and down the road. I was relieved to see them go, so we went on with our plan!

We walked in the house through the back door. I knew that they always left it unlocked. This was Leeper Holler after all. Nobody steals from neighbors around here. I suppose that if they did, they would disappear into the flat woods. And there are a lot of ghosts up there in them flat woods.

And so we went straight away into the bedroom. We got up on Mom and Dad's bed. I tried to stand on

Jimmy's shoulders to unlock the attic door, but that didn't work. So we went to the kitchen and grabbed a chair. As Jimmy steadied the chair on the bed, I climbed up on it and unlocked the attic door. I pulled myself up into the attic, then helped Jimmy up by the hand.

The chair fell off of the bed and hit the floor with a big thump. As we sat there as nervous as a long tailed cat in a room full of rocking chairs, we noticed a light in the corner of the attic. Not needing the flashlights, we tossed them aside by the door. Jimmy with his pistol and me with the machete, we walked over toward the mysterious light.

As we got closer to the light, we could see that it was coming from a trunk on the floor. It was up above where me and Kathy slept. We opened the lid to see what the light was. It looked just like a whirlpool of water, swirling around. Then, we could see in the whirlpool what looked like a magical forest. It was like a magnet pulling us in. As I was being pulled into the trunk, I grabbed Jimmy for help. But it sucked us both in.

Down, down we fell and fell. It seemed like we were falling forever! Finally, we landed on the ground. We stood up, dusted ourselves off, we didn't have a scratch on us! We looked around in amazement! Let me explain what we seen and heard.

There were beautiful mountains reaching up into the heavens. There were mighty pines that seemed to reach God. It was the most beautiful place. We could hear the wind, blowing through the leaves of the trees. We could hear noises in the bushes all around us. And we could hear water flowing in the distance. We had a sense of calm about us. But oddly, at the same time we were a little afraid. We decided to walk toward the sound of the water. As we did, we were very cautious.

As we were getting closer and closer to the sound of the water, we began to see smoke rising up in the air. Someone had a fire going on the bank of the creek. We could feel someone watching us as we approached the water.

Suddenly, we seen a little man with a pipe. He was dressed in green clothes with a funny hat. And he was dancing around the fire. Jimmy looked at me with a very puzzled expression.

"I think that is a Leprechaun little Mac!"

Just then, the little man stopped dancing and looked right at us through the bushes. It was like he could see right through us.

"Come out here, we have been expecting you." He said.

We could hear laughter all around us, but could only see the little man. We came out from hiding behind the bushes. There were logs lined around the fire. The little man said "Come, choose a log and have a seat."

We sat down. The little man began to speak.

"My name is Willy and I'm a Leprechaun. I know that you boys are probably confused right now. Let me try to explain what is going on. You see, this is the world of mystical creatures."

Just then we heard more laughter coming from behind the bushes. Jimmy began to swat at something buzzing around his head.

"No, don't swat at them!" Shouted Willy.

"It's just a big mosquito isn't it?" Said Jimmy.

"No. It's a fairy! And there are many of them here."

And there sure were! They were flying around everywhere. Many of them perched on a log just over from Jimmy and I. And there were many other types of mystical creatures coming out all around us. Willy began naming some of them off. There were Jack-a-lopes, Unicorns, Mermaids and others.

"You see, these creatures that are made up in your world, become a reality in our world. And not just the good ones, but also the bad. Like dragons, griffins, werewolves, ghouls and all kinds of evil beings. But the one I want to talk about, is the one that you brought here with you little Mac."

"I brought one here?" I said.

"Yes! You brought the worst of them all!" Said Willy.

"It is the Rougarou! The legend from Louisiana is that it has the body of a man, with the head of a wolf. Similar to a werewolf, but much stronger and meaner! I have been gathering all of the good creatures, but the Rougarou has been gathering all of the bad ones! There will be a terrible war little Mac, unless you can stop him!

You see, after he destroys our universe, he will go and destroy yours. Until now, he has only been able to visit your attic and a small island on the Black river at night time. But soon enough, he will be more powerful than ever!"

"How can I stop him? I'm only an eight year old boy!"

"You can stop him with something that your Mom told you for a bedtime story little Mac. That is how you will beat the Rougarou!"

Just then, Jimmy jumped up and pulled out his gun.

"I'll help you little Mac! I'll shoot him with this here gun I will!"

"Your gun is useless here." Said Willy.

Jimmy pointed the barrel of the gun to the sky and squeezed the trigger.

"Click."

Nothing happened.

"You see there Jimmy, I told you! It has to be little Mac that defeats him!"

Little Mac looked worried. Willy let out a puff of smoke from his pipe.

"We're gonna leave now little Mac. You are on your own. The Rougarou will be coming soon enough. Remember, all that you need is in your hand and in your heart."

Willy took Jimmy away with him and all of the other mystical creatures followed. Little Mac was afraid. He was trying to remember what it could be that Mom had told him for a bedtime story. What could such a young boy do to defeat a fearful monster? Little Mac cried out:

"Lord, please help me!"

After a few moments, it came to mind! It was the bedtime story of David and Goliath! The young boy who had defeated the giant with only a sling and stones! I had God in my heart and a machete in my hand. So I dropped to my knees and prayed to God.

"Lord, please bless this battle in my favor. Help me to chop this big monster down! Amen."

After getting back up, I heard that same bone chilling cry that I heard before while out on the Black river with my Dad. It was the same terrible howling that had haunted the river for so long. Closer and closer it was coming. But I was not afraid. God was with me in the fight.

The bushes were moving, I could hear it approaching. It pushed over a tree. It made it's appearance stepping out into the light of the campfire. It lifted it's snout to the sky and cried out a terrible howl again. Then I heard God speak.

"When he lets out his war cry, pull your machete back as far as you can, then let it go. Let me guide it to the place it needs to go."

And so I did. As he came right before me, again he reared up and let out his cry. He lifted his huge hairy arm back to swing down his claw. At that moment, I plunged the machete right into his heart. He fell back like a mighty old tree. The Lord had done it! He won the battle!

After he fell to the ground, all the good creatures came out to celebrate! As we were all dancing and cheering in excitement, I heard a quiet voice saying "Wake up little Mac. You are talking and laughing in your sleep."

I knew it was my sweet Mom. I was at home, safe in my bed. She said "You must have been having a good dream!"

I looked at her with a smile as big as Texas across my face.

"Yes I was Mom. Yes I was."

In loving memory of my Mom
Alice Mcfadden
April 28th, 1928 – December 14th, 1984

21

The Story of a Hero

He sits out on the street with a tin cup in his hand. Many pass him by on their way to work every day. But do not even try to understand him. Or why he is even there. They try to look the other way, not to meet eyes with him.

It's hard for them to see the man inside, beneath the rags he wears for clothes. But those who would look deeper, might catch a glimpse of a soldier that fought for our freedom. But in the process, lost his own.

They may even see the hole in his heart, that was put there by a terrible war. Beneath the rugged unkempt beard, the face of a young man that had hopes and dreams of starting a family. But there is no one there for him that cares.

In the midst of the war he was hailed a hero. But now there is no one to even mourn him should he die. A purple heart was given him, but all have forgotten and gone. No, the war is not over for him at all. He now fights it with a bottle, rather than a gun.

It fills his dreams at night. The battles, explosions, the blood running like a river. The visions of his brothers in arms as they violently perished. The haunting of their faces day to day, and a thousand sleepless nights.

A hero though, indeed. Who paid for our freedom with his own. Taking on the nightmares of war, so that we ourselves could sleep safe. A hero, who gave up his dreams, that we might pursue our own.

- To my brother Kenny Mcfadden. I love you bro!

ABOUT THE AUTHOR

Norman Mcfadden is the President of The Glory Riders Motorcycle Ministry, based in Lincoln County, Missouri. A former Pro Wrestler, Norman enjoys hunting and fishing, writing and his various works in Ministry.

Visit Polstonhouse.com today!

The Legends of Leeper Holler Collection

ALSO FROM POLSTON HOUSE

The Legends of Leeper Holler Collection

ALSO FROM POLSTON HOUSE

ALSO FROM POLSTON HOUSE

The Legends of Leeper Holler Collection

ALSO FROM POLSTON HOUSE

www.ingramcontent.com/pod-product-compliance
Lightning Source LLC
LaVergne TN
LVHW050642100826
845148LV00011B/1953

* 9 7 8 1 7 3 3 8 0 8 6 9 9 *